Praise For *Tiger Trouble!*

"Summed up, this is a terrific read for middle graders--girls and boys alike. The characters are simply tons of fun as is the world they live in. There's action, heart-filled moments, tension and humor. Simply said, it's a crazy ninja/agent ride."
-Bookworm for Kids, Book Blog

"This is a very enjoyable read. I bought a copy for my friend's daughter and she LOVED it! There are strong, smart female characters, the book is well paced and well written, and most importantly, it's FUN to read!"
-Amazon Review

"I read the whole book in one day, as I couldn't sleep without knowing what happened, so I got up and finished reading it!"
-Today We Did, Book Blog

"It was super action-packed, witty, fun, and I think a middle grade reader will absolutely love it."
-Cover2CoverBlog

Agent Darcy
&
Ninja Steve
in...
Tiger Trouble!
By Grant Goodman

ISBN-13: 978-1508747161

ISBN-10: 1508747164

Edition 3.2 June 2017

Disclaimer: The following story is a work of fiction. Regarding the events in this book, any similarity to any person, living or dead, is merely coincidental.

This book is dedicated to my parents, my brother, and my students.

Thank you for being awesome.

STEVE

At 6 AM, Ninja Steve was catapulted out of his bed. As Steve shot through the air, he regained his sense of balance, twisted twice, and landed hard on his heels. Without a second thought, he was in a fighting stance, looking for his attacker.

"Happy twelfth birthday, little brother!"

His sister, Ninja Nora, was standing upside-down on the ceiling and laughing so hard she was crying. She had wrapped her black hair into a swirling bun and had stuck two chopsticks through to hold it all in place.

"I can't believe you got me," Ninja Steve said, rubbing his super-short brown hair.

"There's a reason I graduated early from Ninja School," she said, and suddenly she vanished from the ceiling.

Ninja Steve looked all around. She wasn't in the shadows behind the door. She wasn't under the bed.

There was an explosion of wood as Nora burst up through the floor, holding a round, green cake in one hand and a chocolate ice cream cone in the other. She had a huge smile on her face as she threw the ice cream cone at Steve.

The dessert spun end over end. Steve waited until the last second before he cartwheeled to the right. The cone hit the floor and shattered into a thousand pieces. The ice cream landed with a splat. Nora had anticipated his move and was already changing her direction.

Steve dashed to the wall, ran up the side of it, and did a backflip to avoid his sister. He landed with a grunt and Nora had to throw on the brakes. Before she could turn around, he pulled one of the chopsticks out of her hair.

"Hey, no touching the hair!" she shouted, and threw a back-kick that would have sent Steve sailing out of the house if he hadn't dodged it. She really, really hated when people messed with her hair.

Nora rushed after him, bounding from floor to ceiling and back down to the floor in pursuit. Steve wished he had managed to get hold of a smoke bomb or a mist trap or a packet of sneeze dust, but they were all stored neatly in the secret compartment behind his bed. They were the only things that he stored neatly.

Nora touched her finger to the tip of her nose and she became a blur. She circled around Steve again and again at blinding speed and he knew then that there was no escape.

She crushed the entire cake into Steve's face and laughed

out loud as she did it. When Steve finished wiping the green tea icing out of his eyes, he saw that she had *another* cake — this one was white.

"Hey! No fair! You used a level two technique!" Steve shouted. "It isn't even legal for me to use a level one technique!"

"Whatever, snot-face. I'm sixteen and that means I can use any level technique that I want," she said. "You'll start learning some next year and even then you won't stand a chance against me."

Nora reached back, ready to throw the second cake.

The door flew open and Nora froze.

Steve leaped forward and snatched the cake out of her hand.

"What is going on in here?!"

Ninja Steve's parents stood in the doorway. Both of them were dressed for work, so their faces were almost completely covered by their black and gray ninja headgear. Steve's mom was the taller of the two and she stood with her arms crossed.

"Nora attacked me," Steve said, pointing to the cake that was still all over his face.

"It's his birthday!" Nora said. "It's tradition!"

"Enough," their mother said, quietly. "Now, Steve, please hand me the cake you're holding."

Steve hung his head and trudged over to his mother. "It's not fair. I didn't get a chance to strike back."

His mom held out her hands. He handed her the cake.

She smooshed it right into Steve's face.

"Steve, you forget Sensei Raheem's second rule," his father told him. "Say it out loud, please."

Steve sighed. "Never give up your weapon."

His mother nodded. "Correct."

His father said, "Nora, get out of your brother's room. He has to get ready for school and you have to go to archery class now."

Nora huffed and walked out, fixing her hair back in place as she went. She turned and stuck her tongue out at Steve and then disappeared into the hallway. Steve wondered if all sisters were like that.

"Happy birthday, honey," his mother said, with a smile in her voice.

"We'll celebrate after school today, big guy," his father

said.

"Sounds great, dad," Steve said.

His parents left. Steve looked around at his ruined room. The mattress was on its side. His sister had destroyed the floorboards. There was melting ice cream and smeared icing everywhere.

He looked at the clock and saw that he only had fifteen minutes before he had to leave for school.

"Happy birthday to me," he said.

DARCY

Darcy held her breath.

That's what the handbook said you needed to do to calm down when you were hiding from a pursuer. She pressed her back against the wall as hard as she could, as if she could fade into it. In her head, she counted back from ten, just like she had been taught in training.

"…three, two, one."

All she had to do to complete the mission was reach the ship without being caught.

Agent Darcy tucked a loose strand of her black hair back under her baseball cap, turned the corner and started walking as calmly as she could. She walked through the crowded main street and tried to steady her thoughts. She told herself she was prepared for moments like this one. A new plan would have to work. She would find a way to the harbor from the next street over.

Someone tapped her on the shoulder, hard.

Agent Darcy spun around and gasped as she found herself face to face with her assailant, a willowy girl who smiled as she held a stun gun to Darcy's stomach.

"Busted," said Serena, and she flicked Darcy right on the nose. "You fail."

The word hurt her more than the flick on the face. She had done everything according to practice. Her instructors had gone over the best techniques. What more was there to do? How else could you shake someone after you'd been spotted?

"Jeez, you look like you're burning up," Serena said. And then her eyes went wide. "Ohmigod, this is the first test you've ever failed, isn't it?"

Serena was right.

"I...I..." Darcy stammered.

She felt the tears stinging the corners of her eyes. Thirteen years old and now, only now, had she failed a test. The first academic failure of her entire life. The pile of successes, of A's and perfect papers and smiles from her teachers at the Bureau of Sneakery, those had all been wiped away. A single word obliterated every good feeling she'd ever had, replaced all of those triumphs with defeat.

The "f" word.

Fail.

She would not cry in front of Serena. She would *not* cry in front of Serena.

"You are totally about to cry," Serena said, taking off her fedora to let down her long, brown curls. "This is too rich."

Darcy's resolve crumbled and she cried in front of Serena. Serena left the practice zone and from the sound of it, she was skipping. Darcy was leaning back against the wall, patting her eyes with the sleeve of her black combat-ready shirt, wondering when the Lead Agent would dismiss her over the speaker system.

"Agent Darcy, pull yourself together."

Darcy looked up. Leaning over the edge of the roof of one of the fake buildings in this fake town was Lead Agent Evelyn. She, like any good Lead Agent, was average height, with a pretty but indistinct face, and knew how to dress to blend in with the surroundings. Since this was a simulation of a bustling town, she wore a light gray coat, a pair of black gloves, and fashionable but not flashy black boots.

"Yes, ma'am," Darcy said, and sniffled.

She counted backwards from three and took deep, deep breaths. With each decreasing number, she mentally recited a rule from the handbook.

"3: Never make friends with an outsider. 2: Never speak of the Bureau. 1: Never reveal your name to anyone who isn't an agent," she thought, and by then she had steadied herself.

Agent Evelyn used her remote to shut down the practice zone and all of the hologram citizens flickered and disappeared. Aside from where she went in simulations created for the practice zone, Darcy had spent her entire life living in the hidden territory that belonged to the Bureau of Sneakery.

Agent Evelyn leaped from the rooftop and right before she hit the ground, her multi-boots let out a rush of air and she landed gently in front of Darcy. That must have been a new feature developed by The Giga Squad.

"No more crying," Evelyn told Darcy. "It's ill-mannered for an agent of the Bureau of Sneakery."

Darcy looked at her chief instructor. Evelyn had shoulder-length blonde hair and an intense stare that could intimidate anyone. There was a reason she was Lead Agent and it surely wasn't because she was soft. When names were being drawn for mentor agents, Darcy had heard a few others hoping and praying and wishing for anyone other than Lead Agent Evelyn. That had confused her. Shouldn't you want to be trained by the best? Why would anyone settle for less?

Darcy did her best to meet Evelyn's stare and not wither.

"Why did you fail, Agent Darcy?"

"I did not take the right path to the harbor," she said, and the words were heavy coming out of her mouth.

"Wrong," Evelyn said, and Darcy shrank down.

There was a knot in Darcy's chest and it was getting tighter and tighter. Evelyn was trying to get to her, to get under her skin and upset her again. Well, she wouldn't let that happen. She would stick to her answer.

"I...f...failed because I did not take the right—"

Evelyn cleared her throat. "Agent Darcy, repeating the wrong answer does not make it right. Choose your next words carefully."

"I don't know," she said. "I followed the book and the lessons perfectly."

Evelyn smirked. "That is a much better response, agent. When I see you tomorrow, you had better be able to say that word aloud without stumbling around it. The Bureau is all about failure."

With that, Lead Agent Evelyn walked away, down the fake Main Street, and toward one of the many hidden exits in the walls of the practice zone. Darcy went in the opposite direction, out the way she had come in.

She walked out onto campus, which thankfully was mostly empty since it was getting late in the evening. The lamplights were starting to blink on and as she walked the winding path back to her dormitory, she said the word to herself over and over again.

Her room was a rectangle large enough for a twin-size bed, a black desk, a dresser with three drawers, and a closet wide enough for ten hangers. She sat down at her desk and opened up her laptop. Darcy punched in her 20 character password and brought up her writing app.

"I failed today, mom and dad," she said out loud as she typed. "And I will never fail again."

STEVE

Ninja Steve was bored. It was History of the Ninja Wars class and Sensei Raheem was making them all stand on the ceiling while taking notes. Sensei claimed that it would build their endurance. Steve wasn't so sure. All it did was make him want to be right-side-up as soon as possible.

Sensei Raheem was writing on the board using his sword. He was a tall, wide man, bald except for a very short mohawk. In tall, wide letters he wrote the words, "The dinosaur assassins were banished from planet Earth." While the rest of the class was taking notes, Ninja Steve was drawing a picture of a hamburger. He had given it arms and legs, and he was about to give it eyes when he got the strange feeling that someone was behind him.

He turned and found Sensei Raheem standing there, a severe look of disapproval on his face.

"Ninja Steve! Is that a hamburger with arms and legs?"

Steve nodded. "Yes, Sensei."

"Since you clearly don't understand what hamburgers are, I am giving you a week of cafeteria detention. You will be preparing hamburgers for the rest of the ninjas. Except, of course, for the vegetarian ninjas. For them, you will prepare mashed potato patties."

Ninja Steve lost his concentration and fell down from the ceiling. Nothing was more humiliating than cafeteria duty, except for falling off of the ceiling. The other ninja students snickered until Sensei Raheem threw a tomato and hit one of them in the head. It was one of the many weird things Sensei was known for doing.

"Now isn't the time for laughing. The Dinosaur War was serious!" he said, and resumed his lesson.

Steve was sent to the cafeteria ten minutes before the start of lunch.

"You must be my new apprentice for the week," said Sensei Chow. He flared his nostrils after every sentence. Sensei Chow also had the bushiest eyebrows in Ninjastoria. "I already have the food on the grill, but you can serve it."

He handed Ninja Steve a spatula that must have weighed ten pounds.

"You will train hard with that spatula. You will learn that a heavy spatula will make your arms strong and your mind focused. You will learn that mistakes are costly, both in time and energy."

Steve held the spatula tightly as he stood behind the lunch counter. The hamburgers and the mashed potato patties sizzled on the hot grill in front of him. The smell should have made him hungry, but Ninja Steve was nauseous. Any minute now, the cafeteria would fill with the other students and they'd line up for their food. Because every ninja needed to be served lunch, every ninja in the school would know that he had been punished.

The gong struck and lunch began. They all came in, in their black or their white uniforms, talking quietly and occasionally pointing at Steve. Steve flipped the patties onto buns, two at a time. He passed the lunch tray down the line to Sensei Chow, who filled the rest of the plate with fresh berry salad.

"Nice work, Steve," said Samurai Sam when he got to Steve. "What'd you do this time?"

Samurai Sam was the chubby, glasses-wearing son of the Bushido Gardens ambassador. He was also Ninja Steve's best friend.

While everyone else was required to wear the cloth uniforms of the ninja, Samurai Sam was permitted to wear the gray metal armor of his warrior people. It made it easy to find him in the halls, since he was always clanking around with every step. Steve wasn't sure how Sam could stand it, being so noisy all the time.

"I'll tell you later," he said, and Sam moved on.

Getting through the rest of the line took forever. The extra-heavy spatula began to take its toll on Steve and soon his arms felt like they were going to fall off.

"Hey, Steve."

He looked up and it was Ninja Kelly. Steve's hand slipped and the burger he had scooped up fell onto the floor.

"Oh, um, hi," he said, and tried to look cool. But then he couldn't remember how to look cool, so he changed his pose again. "What's up?"

"Nothing much," she said. "I was just wondering wh—"

Before she could finish, Ninja Steph tapped her on the shoulder.

"OH HEY GIRL!" Ninja Steph shouted.

Then they lapsed into girl talk. It was loud and it was energetic and it had absolutely nothing to do with Steve. Ninja Kelly and Ninja Steph continued through the lunch line and didn't look back. Whatever she had been about to tell him was gone forever.

Steve was able to serve himself a burger once everyone else had their food. He took his tray over to the table where Samurai Sam sat, along with Ninja Arjun, who was the tallest ninja student in the whole school. They were talking about the latest episode of their favorite tv show, "Kung-Food."

"Dude, you know that Burrito-San is going to rescue Princess Sashimi next episode, right?" Samurai Sam said.

Arjun shook his head. "That's what they want you to think. Burrito-San is going to get there at the exact same time as Sifu Tofu and they'll spend the whole episode fighting each other. The princess won't be any closer to being rescued."

Steve agreed with Arjun, so all he did was nod. His arms shook as he lifted his burger to take a bite.

"Anyway, Steve, what's up with you today? What happened?" Sam asked.

Steve told them. They laughed at him, because that's what good friends do. He laughed, too. His worries, he realized, were ridiculous. He'd do his lunch prep and then the week would be over and no one would care about it.

Plus, it meant that he had four more chances to talk to

Kelly.

DARCY

Darcy couldn't sleep. She had written a diary entry. She had said goodnight to the photo of her parents. She had listened to her favorite song.

"This is ridiculous," she said into her pillow, and she flopped over onto her side. She was growing frustrated and that definitely wasn't going to help her fall asleep at all. After another minute, she gave up and got up.

The little café in the basement was always open. You never knew when you'd be returning from training, so someone was always there to make sure you didn't have to go to bed hungry. Some of the instructors grumbled that the current students were spoiled and that some missions in the field required going without food and that was how "the real world" worked. Then again, some of the instructors grumbled about everything being better when they were younger.

One of the nice parts of living in a girls-only school was that if you wanted to walk around in your pajamas at night, you could. Darcy wandered downstairs in her powder-blue pajama pants and a white top, passing a handful of other students dressed similarly.

She smelled cinnamon and coffee way before she got to the café. It was music to her nose. When she walked in, all four of the little round tables were empty, their chairs neatly pushed in. One of the glass display cases was open in the back and Matilda was carefully arranging some muffins. She looked out through the glass, saw Darcy, and waved.

Matilda was one of the senior students at the Bureau of Sneakery; she was seventeen. She had a handful of missions to her name, which kept her away from campus most of the time. When Darcy had first entered the Bureau, Matilda had been her guide. Unlike most of the other girls and their mentors, the two of them had stayed friends.

"Darcy, why are you still awake?"

"Bad day," Darcy said.

Matilda closed the case and when she stood up, Darcy saw that she had a spot of powdered sugar on her nose.

"Bad day?" she asked, and brushed the sugar off of her nose. "I've heard of those. A coffee cake muffin is supposed to be a tremendous help."

Darcy shook her head.

"No? Some herbal tea, then?"

"Please."

Matilda poured two cups and then walked over and sat down with Darcy. Darcy stared into her tea and got lost until Matilda cleared her throat.

"If you're not going to drink, then you might as well talk," Matilda said, taking a sip.

Darcy stirred her tea around with a spoon, thinking of where to start. It all seemed so petty. Matilda had been halfway around the world, had probably put her life in danger. What was a training mission gone wrong? It was a waste of Matilda's time.

"It's nothing."

Matilda laughed. "You have got to be kidding me. Out with it, girl."

"You're going to think it's ridiculous. You have real problems, I only have—"

"Whoa. Slow down. This isn't some sort of problem contest. Tell me what's up and you'll feel better."

Darcy told her. It was easier to say this time. She still felt a little ashamed at the end, but not as much as she had expected. And Matilda didn't laugh at all.

"Oh, that's perfectly normal. It doesn't mean you'll never

get your first mission. And, no, they're not going to kick you out for that," Matilda said.

"What?"

"Come on, Darcy. Think about it. Everyone got here by being exceptional. That's all you've been, all the time. Of course it's going to come as a shock when, for once, you mess up. You can't stay perfect forever. None of us do."

Hearing that was a relief, like a rainbow after a storm. Someone else understood.

They talked a lot after that, about the pressure of being in the Bureau, about which class was the hardest, about which agents were training whom. After an hour, Darcy was feeling like herself again.

"Look at you now, girl," Matilda said. "You are a million times better."

"Thanks, Mattie," Darcy told her. "I think I might be able to sleep tonight."

"Go for it," Matilda said. "See you later."

Darcy said goodbye to her friend and walked back through the hall and up the stairs. When she turned the corner to get to her room, she found Lead Agent Evelyn standing there, leaning against the door with her arms crossed. Darcy's good mood suddenly scattered. She knew—absolutely *knew*—that Evelyn was there to kick her out.

"Hello, Darcy," she said. "I wasn't sure if you'd still be awake."

"Hello, Lead Agent," she said.

"We need to talk about something important."

Darcy felt a lump in her throat. She swallowed, and it was still there. "Yes?"

"A mission came up. They needed two candidates. I nominated you."

A mission? Nominated? Now her fear had been replaced by curiosity. What was it? Where was it? How long would it last? A good agent, however, had control, and a good agent wouldn't spout off a stream of questions in the middle of the hallway in the middle of the night. That kind of conduct would get you nowhere.

"Thank you, Lead Agent," was all she said.

"I'll let you ask one question about the mission," Evelyn said. "The rest will have to wait until morning."

There it was. The way to challenge an agent-in-training's

patience. To see how she'd react to having to wait for mission details. She'd win this one.

"Who is the other agent?"

Evelyn cracked a hint of a smile. "Agent Serena."

With that, Evelyn left, and Darcy stood there in the hall, trying to figure out whether she was going to shout with joy or with anger.

STEVE

"A true ninja does not name his katana," said Sensei Raheem, addressing his students as they all stood in the Field of Tall Purple Grass. The grass was tall enough to reach Sensei Raheem's chest. "Just as you do not name your arms, you do not name your katana."

Ninja Steve immediately named his arms. His left arm was Dr. Cyborg and his right arm was Valkor the Great. Why wouldn't you name your arms? That seemed like a cool thing to do.

"Today, you will be practicing the art of precision. Watch carefully."

There was a flash of light as Sensei Raheem drew his katana and returned it to its sheath. He waved his hand and then smiled. The rest of the students looked at each other. What had they missed?

"Sensei, I don't see what—" Ninja Thomas started to say, but Sensei Raheem threw a tomato into his face before he could finish.

"Ninja Steve, tell me what happened," Sensei Raheem

said with crossed arms. "Your sister was the only one in her class who was able to."

Steve hadn't been paying attention. Nora would have and that was why she would have known what Sensei had done. Instead, Steve had been wondering why the grass was purple. Nowhere else in Ninjastoria had purple grass, let alone *tall* purple grass.

"Sensei, you…um…you cut a single blade of grass with your katana," he said.

Sensei Raheem grunted and threw a gold sticker at Steve. It was shaped like a sword and it hit Steve in the middle of his forehead.

"That is for being correct," said Sensei, and Steve glowed with pride. "And this is for not paying attention but still getting a lucky guess."

The tomato came speeding toward his face. Steve leaned to the right and dodged it, only to be hit by a red onion right behind it. Onions, it turned out, hurt far more than tomatoes.

"Now, you will draw your katana once, you will make one cut, and you will trim one blade of grass. Get to work."

The ninjas spread out silently and the purple grass folded

in around them as they settled into new spots. Steve heard the clank of Samurai Sam's armor not too far away. He wanted to talk to Sam, but didn't want to risk another vegetable to the face.

Steve gripped the hilt of his katana, which was a rough sharkskin covered in thin ribbons of silk. His *saya*, the scabbard, was solid black wood. The silver blade he drew was exactly two feet long, stamped with an image of a sunburst just above the *tsuba*, the guard. The katana had been in his mother's family for centuries, dating back at least as far as the Interstellar Pixie Rebellion. Not as far back as the Dinosaur War, though. He would have to find a good, proper name for the sword.

After half an hour of attempts, Ninja Steve was grumpy and sweaty. Sensei had compared him to Nora in front of everyone. So many teachers did that. Steve had lousy test scores, was terrible with any weapon other than a sword, and wasn't interested in most of his classes. Year after year, his teachers mentioned Nora's early admission to college, her deadly accuracy with a blowdart gun in Superbowl XXV, and her decision to double-major in Ghost Studies and Spin Kicks. Nora was, aside from President Ninja, the leading ninja expert on ghosts and was giving monthly lectures at the university. Steve gripped the handle of his sword and stared straight ahead, looking past the grass instead of at it.

He drew his sword slowly, with a long breath. He turned to his right, cut as quickly as he could, and returned his sword to its sheath.

A single stalk of purple grass blew away in the wind. A gold sword sticker from Sensei Raheem hit Steve on his chin before he could even realize what had happened. When he did, he shouted and drew his sword and cut again, convinced he could repeat his task.

Unfortunately, Steve couldn't manage to do it again. Every time, his katana clipped through several blades of grass. The wind was no help, either.

Class was dismissed for lunch. Drawing, swinging, and sheathing a sword so many times had worn everyone out.

Steve had finished his cafeteria duty yesterday and today Sensei Chow was serving lunch on his own.

It was teriyaki chicken with edamame and steamed rice. Ninja Steve's favorite.

"Steve, you have two stickers on you," Samurai Sam said, as they moved down the line. "Where'd the second one come from?"

"I cut the grass," Steve said.

"No way! You did that?"

"I did," he said, and silently thanked his arms, Dr. Cyborg and Valkor the Great.

Someone else joined the conversation. "Really? You cut down a single blade of grass?"

It was Ninja Kelly. She had taken off her hood and let her red hair down. When Steve looked at her, he somehow forgot the basics of how to speak.

"I…grass…yeah," he stammered. Then he got it together. "Yeah, I did."

"Maybe you can help me, then?" she asked.

Steve's brain fired the word "Yes!" about a million times. Thankfully, he only said it out loud once.

"Cool! I can't do tomorrow, but how about Wednesday afternoon? 3 o'clock?" she asked.

Steve smiled a big, stupid smile. "Sure."

"Here, give me your phone," she said and he obeyed.

"Text me, okay?" she said, and then walked off to sit with her friends.

Samurai Sam, who had been standing right next to Steve

the entire time, let out a big breath. "What. Just. Happened?"

Ninja Steve, to whom it had just happened, shrugged. "I have no idea, Sam."

They sat down at the table in silence. Ninja Arjun joined them five minutes later. He looked at Steve, then down at Steve's plate.

"Steve, buddy, are you okay? You haven't eaten," said Arjun.

"Yeah, great. Got to, you know, stuff," Steve said, pushing his rice around with his fork.

Arjun crinkled his forehead. "Steve, you aren't saying anything of value. That didn't make any sense."

Luckily, Samurai Sam was there to translate. "Arjun, five minutes ago, Ninja Kelly gave Steve her number. It's like he's been hit with the spell of a thousand face-slaps."

Arjun laughed. "That would explain it. Steve, you gonna be okay?"

"Yeah, great. Got to, you know, stuff."

"Steve, that still doesn't make any sense," Arjun said. "And if you're not going to eat that, I will."

Ninja Steve pushed his lunch tray over to Arjun and then went back to spacing out. His two friends shrugged and ate. They'd let Steve do his thing and eventually he'd come back down.

Steve couldn't stop thinking about how awesome Wednesday afternoon would be.

DARCY

Darcy couldn't stop thinking about how stressful the afternoon was going to be. She had tried writing in her diary, hoping that turning her stress into words would relieve the pressure.

It hadn't.

She put on her standard agent clothing: black button down shirt, tan pants, black boots. She went to Mission Central, a white marble building in the middle of campus. While most of the buildings had a triangular roof, Mission Central was the only one with a dome. It looked like a big, white bubble. She stood outside the frosted glass double-doors and took a breath. This was it. Her first real assignment.

The handbook said that when you approached Mission Central, you should do it with perfect posture. That if a superior agent passed you, you were to hold open any doors for her to walk through. That if you forgot your agent smartphone, you would not be allowed in.

She touched her agent smartphone to the black box on the side of the door and waited for the little light bulb to blink green. It didn't. She touched her phone to it a second time. Nothing happened.

She started to panic. The handbook said that when your first mission came up, you would automatically be programmed into the system. All you had to do was go to Mission Central and you would be able to get in. It was supposed to be simple.

The third time, the light turned green and the doors slid open with a whisper. A rush of cool air came out as Darcy went in. The overhead lights were a soft yellow.

The lobby was a massive room with a ceiling so high it seemed like it could have been on the moon. She wondered if it was a trick of the light. The only decorations were square red columns that went from floor to ceiling. Darcy counted eight of them.

As she walked, the echoes of her footsteps went on and on and on. Then she remembered that a true agent always takes silent steps and suddenly the room was quiet as a mausoleum.

At the far end of the lobby she came to a tiny desk. The desk was made of white stone and behind it was a woman who might have been older than the stone. She was wrinkly and she was hunched over and she had hair that was as white as ocean foam.

"Good afternoon, lass," she said, with a voice that was full of warmth. "May I see your phone?"

"Yes, ma'am," she said, and handed it over.

"No need to be trembling, dear," she said.

"Yes, well, I'm terribly sorry about that," Darcy said.

The old woman looked at her very carefully. Then she looked at the phone and tapped it against the desk. A screen suddenly appeared in the middle of the white stone desk and it popped up and floated right into the woman's hands. That must have been another one of The Giga Squad's new inventions.

"You are all set now, Darcy," the woman said. "If you could go stand on that clear tile to my left, you'll get to the right place."

"Thank you."

"And, Darcy, you look just like your mother."

"Thank you," Darcy said, though she didn't look at her when she said it. She didn't want to talk about that.

She stood on the clear tile, which was big enough for at least two people to stand on, side-by-side. There was a noise like crickets chirping and then beams of blue light came out from the tile's edges. Darcy's feet were suddenly locked in place and the tile began to turn ninety degrees at a time. The first time it turned, the lobby disappeared. The second time it turned, she could have sworn she was looking at her childhood bedroom. The third turn put her in a room full of vases and statues. The fourth turn put her in a wallpapered room with large, comfy chairs, a glass cabinet full of jewelry, and a roaring fireplace.

She didn't like the way the room looked. And she didn't like how the room had Serena in it.

"Oh, look, it's Darcy," Serena said from where she stood by the fireplace. "I wonder if she's going to cry this time, too."

Darcy shook her head and didn't respond. She wouldn't rise to Serena's goading. She would let it roll off.

"It's okay, Darcy, I don't want to work with you, either. I was hoping my first mission would be solo," she said, twirling her hair in her fingers.

Serena leaned against the mantelpiece and was about to say something else when the entire fireplace began to lift off the ground. She lost her balance and fell over. The fireplace was a secret doorway and Lead Agent Evelyn walked through, right beside a woman Darcy had never seen before.

She wore a black dress and her hair was in braids. When this woman saw Serena still trying to get up, she laughed at her. Darcy liked this woman a lot.

Evelyn made the introduction. "Agent Darcy and Agent Serena, this is Commander Natalya."

Darcy stood up straighter. In the Bureau of Sneakery, Commanders were above the Lead Agents, though they were below the Director.

"At least one of you has the manners to stand," Natalya said. "Thank you."

Serena's face had turned a deep, deep red. This was going much better than Darcy had expected.

"For now, though, find a chair, so we can discuss details."

The two girls seated themselves and Natalya touched a button above the fireplace-door. The painting above the fire — a controlled mess of lines and circles — became a display screen.

"I'm sure both of you are familiar with Ninjastoria," said Natalya. "We have a student exchange with them every year. They send two of their top ninjas to our campus, we send two of ours to their city. It lasts six months and then everyone goes home."

Darcy nodded. She had seen the ninja girls last year. They always moved so quickly.

Natalya continued. "The exchange is also a long-running

contest between us and them. Each pair of students has one task to complete during their stay. The first team to successfully do it receives a ranking promotion. Of all of our students, you two are our top nominees."

The girls looked at each other with even, stoic faces. Darcy couldn't stand Serena, but she did know that Serena was a very talented agent. It was a grudging admission, though it was true. If anyone was her number one competition, it was her.

"What kind of task?" asked Darcy.

"Tough stuff," said Natalya. "In the past it's been helping old ladies cross the street, inflating balloons, or getting a kiss."

Then she broke into laughter. "Kidding, of course. We can't tell you until you're on campus."

"An exchange student contest?" said Serena. "*That's* our mission?"

Natalya sighed. "You should take this more seriously. It's not like we're sending you to summer camp. Besides, our agents have won the contest nine years in a row. I'm sure you two will make it ten, no problem."

That seemed to settle Serena. And it made Darcy feel a spark of excitement.

"You have the next two hours to pack and then you're off. Someone will come to get you from your dorm room."

Natalya snapped her fingers and the screen turned back into a painting.

"Here are your agent watches," she said, handing one to Darcy, then to Serena.

Darcy couldn't help but smile. It was the sign of a true agent. While it looked like a regular watch, it had many extra features that would be unlocked with each promotion. Darcy's had a thin, rectangular watch face and a strap made of soft, brown leather.

"You'll need new names for the mission," Natalya said. "So we picked them out for you. Agent Serena, you will be going by the name 'Ashlyn.'"

Serena nodded.

Evelyn looked at Darcy. "Agent Darcy, you will change your name to 'Marcy.'"

Darcy frowned. "May I ask you a question?"

Evelyn glared at her. "It seems like you just did. Ask another."

Darcy's mouth went dry. "Isn't…isn't that a little close to

my real name?"

"No," Evelyn said, and that was that.

"Okay, agents, that is all for now," said Natalya. "The elevator tile will take you out of here."

Natalya pressed a button and the hidden doorway sprang open and she walked away. Lead Agent Evelyn trailed after her.

Serena looked at Darcy and shrugged. "That wasn't what I was expecting."

For once, Darcy agreed with her.

STEVE

"Dude, we're getting two exchange students," Arjun said. He was holding a red target pad high in the air.

Ninja Steve threw a roundhouse kick. It made a satisfying *"pop!"* when he hit the pad. Before the sound had died, Steve had already reset and kicked with his other leg.

"New students? That's no big deal," Steve said quietly. He was trying to stay on Sensei Raheem's good side. Earlier in the day, he had actually paid attention during History of the Ninja Wars. He even took notes on the inter-dimensional skirmish with the Pluton People.

"Sam told me he's pretty sure they're both girls," Arjun said.

Steve threw another kick, heard another "pop" from the pad. A bead of sweat rolled down the side of his face before the lower part of his cloth mask absorbed it. He was almost finished, only six more kicks to go.

"So what?" Steve asked. "I'm seeing Kelly tomorrow."

Even though he said it, he still couldn't believe it. The thought gave him more energy and he started kicking even harder.

"Come on, Arjun, it's no big deal," Steve said, mid-kick. "It's two girls. We should probably stop talking about—"

Arjun's eyes suddenly went wide. That was when Steve knew that Sensei Raheem was standing somewhere behind him.

"Ninja Steve," said Sensei. "You can talk about girls later today."

"Yes, Sensei."

"*Much* later. Because now you need to add in two hundred more kicks." Sensei Raheem laughed and gave himself a high-five before walking away. "You too, Ninja Arjun."

They both sighed and Steve started kicking again. When the work was done, they were the last ones on the training field, which was out in the open. The sun was dipping low and the grass was turning gold-green. Steve sat down and did leg stretches.

"That sucked," Arjun said. "Remind me to keep my big mouth shut next time."

"I tried," said Steve.

They walked home after that. Arjun's house was on the same street as Steve's. They didn't say much. They were too tired and still a little angry at each other.

Steve walked in the front door and took off his tabi boots. He yawned.

Then, Nora leaped at him and shouted something he couldn't quite understand.

Steve wanted to shout back at her. He couldn't, though. There was a terrible itch in his nose. He sneezed. Sneezed again. And again. And five more times after that.

When it was done, his entire body hurt from sneezing so much. What had happened? Was it ninja allergies? One time, Steve had met a kid who was allergic to throwing stars. Was that happening to *him* now?

There was a burst of smoke and when it cleared, Nora was standing right in front of him with her hands on her hips. "Ha! That was a new spell I invented! How was it?"

"Awful."

She clapped. "Yes! That is the spell of eight sneezes."

"Is it a level two spell? Or is that a level three?" Steve asked.

"Level one is illusion, level two is physical effect, and level three is harm," Nora said. "I guess it's a level two point five, maybe a three...depending on how hard the victim sneezes."

Steve nodded. That was a powerful spell to command. It was even more distracting than the other spell she had invented: the spell of three burps. At least if he was burping, Steve could fight back.

This time, he waited until Nora seemed happy enough, and then he charged. She slipped away, quick as the wind, and suddenly she was in the next room. Steve saw her land on the dining room table, which was breaking a huge house rule. Rules weren't on his mind, though, so he jumped onto the table, too.

Even though his leg muscles were worn out, he threw a roundhouse kick at her head. Nora ducked under it. The moment his foot touched back down, he threw a sidekick and caught her on the shin.

"You're getting sloppy, Nora!" he shouted.

"And you're getting off that table!" his dad said from the doorway.

They both froze and slowly turned to face their father.

"Someone needs to start talking," he said.

Steve spoke as fast as he could. "Nora cast a spell on me and then ran away."

"What spell?" their dad asked.

Nora didn't seem so proud of it anymore. "The spell of eight sneezes. It only works on people so--"

"You know the rules about spells in the kitchen, Nora. So here's one from me: the spell of grounded for the rest of the week."

Steve laughed. "That's what you deserve."

"You're standing on the table, Steve. So that means you're grounded tonight and tomorrow."

"But, Dad, tomorrow I'm—"

His father clapped his hands and booming thunder erupted. "No more words."

Steve was stunned. What was he going to tell Kelly? What if he never got another chance? It wasn't fair. It was all Nora's fault, anyway.

Steve sat in his room and thought of what he would do to get even. He would fill her tabi boots with cement. He would swap her super-sharp throwing stars for dull ones. He would dip her ninja mask in hot pepper oil.

He was going to get her back for this.

DARCY

The lobby was completely empty as Darcy and Serena left Mission Central. That old lady had gone and her desk had vanished, too. Maybe there was a camouflage field over it?

They were halfway across the lobby when a piercing alarm went off. A thick, steel plate came crashing down over the front door, trapping them inside. The red columns in the lobby began to glow brighter and brighter.

"What's going on?" said Serena. "My watch is dead."

Darcy wasn't listening to Serena. Darcy was staring at the masked figure in the corner of the lobby. A dull gray mask with three red slashes across the left cheek. He…or was it a she? Whoever it was walked forward very slowly, very deliberately.

"Serena, we need to go," Darcy said.

By then, Serena had noticed, too. They both backed up to where the transport tiles were, only this time, the tiles weren't active. There was nowhere left to go but backwards.

"I don't have a weapon," Serena quietly said.

"Me neither."

The alarm began to blare even louder. Darcy wanted to cover her ears and crouch down until it all went away. That wasn't an option, though.

"Good evening," said the masked man. The voice definitely belonged to a man. "How are you?"

Neither of them spoke a word. The transport tiles blinked to life. They filled with light and began to spin. And when they stopped, Evelyn came flying out with Natalya following right behind her. The masked man stood completely still.

"Hello, sweetheart," he said, though Darcy couldn't tell if he was speaking to Evelyn or Natalya.

Evelyn's jump-kick struck him in the center of his chest. He didn't budge. She hopped back just in time for Natalya to throw a stun dagger. He reached out and caught it with a bare hand. Purple lightning bloomed from the dagger and coursed up his arm. Any normal person would have been knocked unconscious. Whoever this guy was, it didn't bother him at all.

"I only want to talk," he said, and dropped the dagger. It clattered against the floor.

Evelyn had retreated until she stood in front of the girls. "Get onto the transport tile."

Darcy didn't need to be told twice. She and Serena quickly stepped onto the platform and it began to turn. The first rotation put them in a classroom. The second rotation put them onto a snowy mountaintop. The third rotation put them in some kind of aquarium. And the final stop put them in a room with no windows.

"What is going on?" Serena asked.

"Something is really, *really* wrong," Darcy said.

"Do you recognize where we are?" Serena asked.

Darcy shook her head. She was breathing heavily and she kept darting her eyes around, as if the masked man would somehow walk through the walls and reappear. Based on what she had seen a few moments ago, Darcy hadn't ruled it out as a possibility.

"I'm never going anywhere without a weapon again," said Serena, and Darcy agreed.

Neither of their watches were working. Darcy wasn't sure if it had been ten minutes or ten hours by the time Evelyn finally materialized inside the room. All she knew was that she felt safer with Evelyn nearby.

"It's okay now," Evelyn said. She had a cut on her neck

and another on the back of her right hand.

The tone in her voice, though, told Darcy that maybe it wasn't really okay. Maybe it was only going to be okay for a little while.

"What just happened?" Darcy asked. "Who was that?"

Evelyn shook her head. "I can't tell you that right now."

"Well, when *can* you?" Serena said.

Evelyn scowled. "Don't speak to me like that, agent."

Serena shut up immediately. Darcy made a note to practice using those words and that tone. It might come in handy in the future.

They all stood there in silence. Darcy wanted to talk more, but every time she saw Evelyn's expression, she knew it was a bad idea. While Evelyn was on high alert, Serena had gone completely pale. Darcy wondered if that was how she looked, too.

"Okay, let's go now," Evelyn said, apparently picking up on some private signal or message.

"Where? This place is all walls," Serena said.

Evelyn touched one part of the wall and a tiny patch of

green light appeared. She scanned her fingerprints one by one and then the entire wall melted away. They all exited into a narrow steel staircase that went up and up and up. Darcy's leg muscles started to burn.

When they reached the end of the stairs, they emerged from the trunk of a gigantic tree in the woods. She realized that they had been whisked away into some sort of emergency shelter, cut off from the rest of campus. Once Darcy got her bearings, she figured out that it was on the very edge of campus, out past even the most distant training facility.

"We have to go to the Command Post," Evelyn said.

The girls nodded and followed her.

The Command Post was a tower and it took them half an hour to reach it. When they walked in, it was full of agents on the move. Evelyn moved through the crowd and through a locked door into a hallway that was completely empty.

They walked into a room and found Commander Natalya there. While she wasn't *physically* injured, she still looked like she had been badly hurt.

"We need to talk," she said. "And then you have to go."

STEVE

Steve begged his father to reconsider his decision to ground him. Steve did the unthinkable and told him about his afternoon with Kelly. Steve had never talked to his father about stuff like that. After all, what would his dad know about dates?

Then again, Steve didn't know if it was actually a date or not. He knew that ninja dates tended to involve rooftop running, smoke bomb throwing, and dagger sharpening. Oh, and tea. That was standard stuff, right there. Pretty much every girl in Ninjastoria was into those things.

His father took a few hours to think while Steve sat in his room, reorganizing his smoke bombs by color. Nora had broken into his room in the morning and mixed them up. Now he needed to sort them according to Sensei Raheem's system. Misty nights needed the light gray ones, stormy nights needed charcoal, moonless nights needed solid black. Steve also had a few fun ones in blue and in yellow. They were great for big events, like the Festival of the Talking Lobsters or the Moon-in-the-Water Parade.

There was a knock on the door. His dad walked in.

"Steve," he said. "I've thought it over."

A tightness gripped Steve's chest.

"You are ungrounded for—"

Steve did a backflip. He landed and punched his fist in the air.

"Dad, you are the best!" he said, and they fist-bumped.

"You didn't let me finish," his dad said. "You're ungrounded for today but you are re-grounded tomorrow. I don't want my son missing out on an afternoon with the girl he has a crush on."

"Dad, you don't have to say it so loud," Steve said.

Nora yelled something from the other room. Steve knew that she had heard everything. Now he'd never hear the end of it.

"You should probably get going soon, Steve. The Field of Tall Purple Grass is a good ways away. Great choice for a date, that place is very romantic."

"Dad, please stop talking," Steve said, hitting his palm against his own head.

"Fine," he said, and left.

Steve picked up his katana and then he ran. He ran past

The Great Wall of Mart, which was having a sale on grappling hooks. He ran past ShuriKen's Steakhouse, which had recently turned its menu all vegetarian. He ran past Tae Kwon Donuts, which had a line going out the door.

He reached the Field of Tall Purple Grass at 2:45, fifteen minutes before Kelly was supposed to arrive. He slowed his breathing using the Six Steps of Calm Wind. Once he was good, he leaned up against a tree and watched the grass wave in the wind.

Steve already knew what he'd say to her. He'd look at her and say, "You look great today."

There had been a huge brainstorming session. He had thought about using "How's your afternoon been?" and then decided against it in favor of "Is that a new sword?" and then discarded *that* in favor of a simple "How are you?" All of that had been exhausting and he went through about a hundred more ideas before settling on the current one.

Steve snapped out of his thoughts and realized that she was running late. The general rule of the ninjas was that running late was dangerous. It wasn't acceptable for a mission and therefore it wasn't acceptable for real life.

He got out his phone and saw that he had left it on stealth

mode, which made it not only silent, but also invisible. He flipped the switch and immediately saw there was a message from Kelly, sent 20 minutes ago.

"I can't make it. Sorry."

Steve sighed and sat down in the tall purple grass. Of course she wouldn't come out. Not with him. Maybe with someone super cool like Ninja Leo or Ninja J.T. Those guys had all the luck.

He was busy sulking and feeling sorry for himself when he heard two people walking by.

"...this can't be right," one of them said.

"I'm pretty sure we shouldn't be anywhere near a field of high, violet grass," said the other.

There were two girls walking through the Field of Tall Purple Grass, and judging by the fact that they were lost, they clearly were not ninjas. One of them, the tall one with light brown curly hair, was wearing a white button-down shirt. The other one was too short to see in the tall purple grass.

"This isn't right. We should go back," the short one said from somewhere in the grass.

"I think you chose the wrong way in that mirror maze,"

the tall one said.

Steve nodded. The mirror maze was an incredibly tricky thing to navigate. It had been built over five thousand years ago by Head Ninja Phillip III, who was a lover of puzzles. He had installed a three mile wide maze of mirrored panels that rotated every two weeks. According to the history books, no one really liked Head Ninja Phillip III, not even his mother. Despite his lack of popularity, however, the maze remained.

Steve stood up and waved. "Hi! I can help you out."

The tall girl turned and frowned. "Oh my god, have you been listening to us this entire time?"

Steve thought she was as pretty as Ninja Kelly, but she wasn't exactly giving him a great first impression. Her attitude, he realized, had suddenly imitated his sister's.

"Please ignore her," said the shorter girl, who stepped out into a shorter patch of grass.

"I...um...I guess I can do that," Steve said, smiling.

She was in a black t-shirt, black pants, and black boots. Immediately, Steve liked her style. The fact that she had black hair didn't hurt, either. Ninjas were partial to the color black. She had freckles, too, and while not all ninjas were partial to freckles,

Ninja Steve was.

"Thank you. I'm Marcy, this is Ashlyn. We're exchange students," she said, extending her hand.

They shook and she nearly crushed his hand. He offered his hand to Ashlyn, who looked at him and crossed her arms. Fine, he could deal with her for a few minutes. Unlike Nora, he knew he didn't have to live with her.

"I'm Ninja Steve," he said, and couldn't think of anything else to say to them.

"I think the mirror maze put us in the wrong direction," Marcy said. "We're supposed to be meeting Sensei Apple at the fountain."

"Oh, no problem," Steve said. "The mirror maze changes every two weeks, but there are only six possible patterns."

Ashlyn rolled her eyes. "You have got to be kidding me. It changes all the time? And it's in the very center of the village?"

"Yeah, Head Ninja Phillip III—the guy who ordered to have it built—was kind of a jerk," Steve told them, and Marcy laughed.

As they walked, he let them know about Phillip's greatest hits and misses: how he had funded the research that eventually created the exploding pineapple (a clear hit) and how he had outlawed fries for a period of six months (a huge miss).

"Anyway, where are you two coming from?" Steve asked.

"We're from The Valley of Fallen Stars," Ashlyn said.

Steve nodded. He had never met anyone from so far away. The Valley of Fallen Stars was *way* in the north, past Fancy Plains, beyond Hailstorm Heights, and across the sprawling Lake of the Silver Lady. There was a powerful magic in that place, one which drew all falling stars to land in the valley. While Ninjastoria was devoted to studying the arts of stealth and combat, those who lived in The Valley of Fallen Stars were supposed to be trained in a kind of astro-magic that could control a fallen star.

"That's so cool. I've never seen a fallen star up close," Steve said.

As if on cue, Marcy reached into her pocket and pulled out a shiny silver and black piece of metal. It was lumpy and uneven, each part of it shining in a different way. She held it out and put it in Steve's hand. It was heavier than he thought it would be, and it was colder than he thought it could be. His mind could only focus on how amazing it was to hold it: the stars were pinned in space and they burned hotter than any fire.

According to Sensei Raheem, not even the spell of dragon breath could rival the heat of the stars. And no one was sure what caused the stars to fall from the sky.

Now he was holding one in his hands.

"It's not that special," Ashlyn said. "You don't have to drool over it."

"Oh, sorry," Steve said, and handed the star back to Marcy.

Marcy looked at Ashlyn and shook her head. "It *is* special. They don't get them here in Ninjastoria."

She turned to Steve and smiled, which made him feel a sudden warmth in his face. "Don't mind her, Steve. We've had a long day and we got lost."

He nodded. "No worries."

They had arrived at the mirror maze. Hundred-foot high panels formed the walls, some of them square, some of them rectangular, some of them triangular. It looked like someone had destroyed a giant's mirror and then randomly glued the pieces back together. Steve knew that some ninjas would use their flying kites to go above it all. Most ninjas, however, took pride in memorizing the patterns of the mirror maze.

When they entered, the mirror maze was full of ninjas, most of whom were using lightning-step technique and were moving so fast they had turned into blurs.

"Welcome back to the mirror maze," he told them, and checked his reflection to make sure his uniform looked good.

DARCY

"It's not weird," Darcy told Serena once they were alone. "To them, it's perfectly normal."

"Why would anyone build a giant labyrinth made of mirrors? And why would they choose to keep it for centuries? The whole thing gets in the way of getting places. *Our* campus isn't weird like this."

"Our campus has entire sections that are replicas of towns. We fill them with hologram people and sneak after them. Are you telling me that's not weird?"

Serena huffed and went back to unpacking her stuff. They were, to Darcy's horror, sharing a room. Their host family, Ninja Morris and Ninja Gertie, had let them in and shown them to their room right away. It was much wider than Darcy's cramped room at the Bureau, though the ceiling was much lower. Thankfully, they didn't have bunk beds. In fact, they didn't have beds at all.

Apparently, Morris and Gertie were old-school ninjas who believed in bed rolls—thin mattress pads that you put out when you were sleeping and then rolled up and stashed away during the day. Darcy had grown used to her tough mattress at the Bureau and assumed that sleeping only a few inches away from the floor wouldn't be all that different.

Serena was moving a jacket into a closet when a slip of paper fell free and floated halfway across the room before sliding to a halt at Darcy's feet. She didn't mean to look at it, but there was no avoiding it...the photograph had landed face up. It was a much younger Serena with a bright blue bow in her hair, wearing a darker blue dress. On either side were her parents. There was no denying that the woman to the left was her mother: their hair was the same, their smiles were the same, even their rounded noses were the same. The man, who must have been her father, was stick-thin, which was where Serena must have gotten it from.

Darcy handed it back, a little embarrassed, as if she had glimpsed a secret she was never meant to know about.

"When did you last hear from them?" Darcy asked.

It was a common question among agents. To be an agent in training meant going months at a time without contacting anyone.

"It's been a while," she said, staring at the photo. "You?"

"Same," Darcy said.

She went back to unpacking her own stuff. Her laptop, her e-reader. She hung up her four black shirts, her lone white shirt, her pants. The rest of her clothes went in the built-in shelves in the other half of the closet. Her two pairs of multi-boots (one brown, one black) were placed side by side. They were the newest model: not only could they grip onto surfaces, they could cushion a big fall with a big burst of air if she pressed the proper button on her watch.

Tomorrow would be their first day of school.

In a new place.

Where they didn't know anyone.

Well, they knew Ninja Steve. Darcy knew she wasn't supposed to be nervous. An agent's job was to go to strange places and blend in. Of course, their world had all kinds of weird corners and blending in wasn't always easy. There was The Mole Republic, for starters.

That night, they lay on their bed rolls, both wide awake, not saying anything. Darcy didn't want to be the first to speak because she didn't want Serena to know she was anxious. She was pretty sure Serena was thinking the same thing.

There was also the matter of the incident at Mission Central. And the meeting that followed.

Darcy had only been partially listening to the commander. Something about a break-in, something about hidden documents or technology. That everything was under control. Now it all seemed like a distant dream. She had been too freaked out to really make sense of any of it.

Ordinarily, she would have written in her diary. With Serena in the same room, however, she didn't even try to pull up her writing app. If she found out about Darcy's diary…

When Darcy finally fell asleep, she didn't dream.

Her watch—which was also her alarm—rang at 5:30. Serena's rang at the same time. They both sat up and rubbed their eyes and double checked their watches, as if both of them could be wrong.

"I'm taking the first shower," Serena said, and had grabbed her towel and walked off before Darcy could reply.

They had a tiny bathroom across from their room with a shower that was meant to fit half a person.

Darcy put on her watch and tapped the middle of the screen. It activated her wireless connection to the SpyNet. She picked up her phone and checked her email. Nothing new.

They both arrived on the school grounds as the sun rose,

each carrying a backpack that held a laptop, a few pencils and pens, and a folder full of paper. All around them, ninja students rushed by, most wearing all-black uniforms. Only a few of them stopped to stare or point at the new girls.

The campus looked more like an obstacle course than an educational facility. The students were climbing steel bars built onto the sides of the buildings, then zip-lining from rooftop to rooftop. Others were leaping off of rooftops, using gliders that sprouted from somewhere in their uniforms. Some students were hopping out of windows onto a series of tall, wooden poles that led to another set of windows.

"They'd better have stairs," said Serena.

They didn't.

When they finally found the entrance to Katana Hall, where there should have been a staircase, there was a big hole. It was at least a ten foot drop. Darcy gulped. Most of the time, they would have used their gear to navigate situations like these. But they were under special instructions not to use their multi-boots unless they were completing their task for the competition.

"What are you two waiting for?" said one of the ninja girls. "It's only a short jump."

The ninja girl stepped forward, jumped down, and rolled

the moment her feet touched. Darcy stepped right up to the edge and before she could think, she jumped. The fall was faster than she anticipated and when she hit, she only had a split second to shift the weight off of her feet as she collapsed into a roll.

Serena landed soon after. "That was crazy. How do you get back up?"

Another ninja came running down the hallway. He leaped, kicked off the side of the wall, and made it onto the upper landing. Then he turned back and yelled, "There are climbing rungs on the side!"

Darcy looked and saw them embedded into the wall. They would have been impossible to spot from up top. At the very least, that would make things easier.

They entered the classroom and it was silent. No desks, no electronic display board, and not a single student was wearing a backpack. Some of the ninjas were still milling around. Darcy was glad to see that it was a small class. She didn't know much about swords. The agency was more about guns than blades.

"Oh, hey Marcy."

It was Ninja Steve. He spoke quietly and when he did, the rest of the class shifted their attention. Darcy tried to ignore them, to forget that there were so many eyes watching her.

"And...um..." he said, looking at Serena. "Sorry, but I guess I forgot your name."

"Whatever, I forgot your name, too," Serena said. "I'm Ashlyn."

"Right, I'm Steve. Anyway, how's everything going so far?" he asked.

"I'm not sure where to start," Darcy said. "Things are different here. But the soup we had last night was amazing."

"Ninja Gertie's curry udon is real serious business," Steve said. "She's won the Soup Olympics for the past thirty years."

Darcy laughed. "A Soup Olympics?"

Surely, Steve was joking.

"Oh yeah, it's a big event. The World Series of Tempura is next month."

"I think I'm going to enjoy that," she said.

Maybe, she thought, Ninjastoria was a place she could grow to like.

STEVE

"Ninja Steve, get over here," Sensei Raheem said.

Steve felt his stomach turn into a pit full of rocks. He walked forward and tried to keep his head held high. Luckily, he didn't tremble in front of a crowd anymore, like he used to.

"Now, class, observe the way Steve draws his katana," Sensei Raheem said.

Steve dropped his right hand to his side. He took a breath. He heard his father's voice in his head: *pull straight and true and your blade will become like the wind. The wind doesn't think and it doesn't hesitate. The wind is there and then it isn't.*

Steve held his position. Sensei Raheem nodded.

"On three," Sensei Raheem started. "One. Two."

The ground lurched. Steve wobbled.

The ground split open. Steve fell.

His instincts took over.

On the way down, he sheathed his sword and made sure he was right side-up, ready to deal with the impact. There was a red light coming from below and Steve braced for landing. He hit the gravel-covered bottom and broke into a roll to the side.

Steve got up and brushed some gravel off of his arms. He wished now that he hadn't worn his short sleeve black ninja shirt. Some of the rocks had dug deep into his skin.

The air he breathed was thick and smoky. The soft red light came from everywhere and nowhere at once. No matter which direction he moved in, he couldn't track the source of it.

"Dig, dig, dig, dig!" he heard someone shouting.

Steve looked through the red glow and saw the outline of something in the distance, something that looked like a parade. He moved toward it, his hand on his sword hilt. The gravel crunched beneath his boots and with each step, a mist began to rise up from the ground.

There was a crash from behind. Steve whipped his head around and tried to figure out what had happened, but the mist had become too thick. Instead, he kept moving toward the silhouettes. The cavern was beginning to heat up and Steve felt sweat forming on his forehead.

"Steve! Where are you?"

Sensei Raheem's booming voice was unmistakable.

"This way!" Steve yelled.

The voices ahead grew louder, more panicked. "Dig, dig, dig!"

"Sensei, what is that?"

Sensei Raheem furrowed his brows. "From the sounds of it, Steve, I think we're dealing with a pack of scout mecha-moles."

Steve shook his head. "What?"

"They're from The Mole Republic, Steve. There are scout mecha-moles, brute mecha-moles, and royal mecha-moles. I had to deal with them when I fought the Mole Emperor all those years ago. The fact that they're here now isn't good."

"So what do we do?"

"Steve, we kick their butts."

"Okay, I guess we—"

"I mean it literally, Steve. Scout mecha-mole bodies are tough, almost like armor. Their only weak point is the butt. You *must* kick their butts."

With that, Sensei Raheem, legendary hero of Ninjastoria, charged down the tunnel. Steve followed after him. The pack of mecha-moles was waiting for them. They were each close to three feet high and ranged in color from forest green to neon green. They had tiny, black eyes and sharp, pointed snouts. Their wide, clawed hands were coated in a silvery metal and black cables went from their wrists to their elbows. Their mecha-claws were covered in dirt and gravel.

Steve went to draw his sword and all five mecha-moles stood up. Their noses twitched and they raised their claws above their heads.

"Steve! Don't draw your sword! The mecha-moles eat steel! It's like pizza to them!" Sensei Raheem yelled. "Weren't you listening earlier?! KICK! THEIR! BUTTS!"

The mecha-moles began to advance. They kept their claws raised and their heads down and Steve wasn't sure if he was about to fight or about to be in a very strange music video. Then one of them slashed its claws at his face.

He dodged another claw swipe and lunged to the side. The mecha-mole was slow to turn and Steve threw a spinning roundhouse kick that struck it right on its behind. The mecha-mole went flying through the air and crashed into another. As soon as they recovered they both began digging into the ground.

Sensei Raheem was busy fighting the other three. He was a whirling, flipping, martial-arts tornado and he seemed to be everywhere at once. The first mecha-mole received a heel kick and went spinning into the air before hitting a wall. The second mecha-mole came bursting out of the ground right behind Sensei Raheem, and somehow he dropped onto his stomach to dodge and then did a reverse rocket kick. Steve guessed that that particular mecha-mole wouldn't be able to walk right for at least a week.

The final mecha-mole realized that it was the only one that wasn't digging its way to safety. It quickly changed that.

"Sensei, they're all escaping!"

Sensei Raheem nodded and threw a tomato at the last escapee, hitting it square on the butt. "Yes, Steve, that much is obvious."

"Why are you letting them get away?"

"Mecha-moles are excellent tunnelers. We could never catch up with them. For now, let's get out of here."

He ushered Steve back to where the hole in the ground had opened up. He pulled out two grappling hook launchers. They blasted their grappling hooks into the sides of the rocks and began to climb. Halfway there, Sensei Raheem grabbed Steve by the wrist and hurled him up into the air. Steve flew the rest of the way.

When Steve landed, the class flocked around him. Everyone was asking a question or pushing their way toward him. Everyone, that was, except for Marcy and Ashlyn.

"What was down there? It sounded like a fight!"

"Did you find treasure?"

"Was it a dragon's lair?"

Sensei Raheem came leaping out of the tunnel and landed with a heavy thud. The class scattered at once. Steve let out a sigh of relief, because had had no idea what to say to anyone.

"When I asked Steve to demonstrate, I had a sinking feeling about it," Sensei Raheem said, and everyone groaned. "It looks like Steve uncovered a hidden tunnel from long ago. I have to cancel class and find a team of explorers to go down there and figure out where it leads. We're done for today."

The reaction was mixed. Steve, however, was disappointed. Of all his classes, Katana Class was his favorite. It was the one time he felt like he really knew what he was doing.

"Ninja Steve, a moment, please," Sensei Raheem said, as the last of the students filed out. "What you saw today was serious. We have invaders in our territory. If word gets out in the wrong way, it might cause a panic. Do you understand what

I'm saying?"

"Yes, Sensei," Steve said, and bowed.

"Good. And, Steve, nice technique down there. I saw that kick."

"Thank you, Sensei," Steve said.

The moment Steve left the classroom, he pumped his fist in the air a bunch of times. Another compliment from Sensei Raheem! Maybe school wasn't so bad, after all. He jumped into the air and was about to shout something happy when he realized he wasn't alone in the hallway.

Marcy and Ashlyn were there, too, and they were both giggling.

DARCY

Darcy stopped taking her laptop to classes. None of the classrooms had internet access. The entire village, it turned out, had limited internet, had almost no wifi. She had never realized that schools could be built without internet access. And she never would have dreamed that an entire society of people could exist without a constant link to Worldopedia or MeTube.

If it wasn't for her agent watch, she would have been completely cut off from the rest of the Bureau when she was in her room. The watch was active now, feeding her a connection and letting her video chat with Matilda.

"That sounds crazy," Matilda said, as she rolled out the dough for her croissants. "Almost every hallway is an obstacle course?"

"Pretty much," Darcy said. Going from class to class was a workout. Her legs were still sore from yesterday, when she finally attempted to jump from post to post in order to get from Ninja Geometry to the smoke bomb laboratory. It was mostly a success, except for the last jump, where she landed funny and almost broke an arm.

"Okay, so, last thing before I go. Tell me about the boys!"

Matilda said, with a wink.

"Oh, um…" Darcy stammered. What could she say? They looked her way from time to time. Many of them wore full masks, though, so she never saw their faces. And most of them were silent.

"What? Come on, Darcy. It's me you're talking to," Matilda said.

"I haven't really met anyone here other than Ninja Steve," Darcy said.

"Oh? His name is Steve?"

Darcy blushed. "It's not like that, Mattie! He's nice to me, but it's…it's not like that."

"Okay, okay. Relax. As long as someone over there is being nice to you, that's all I care about."

"Thank you. It's time for me to get some homework done. I have to write about their war with The Mole Republic. I swear, the ninjas have had more wars than anyone else in the land."

"Good luck with all that," Matilda said. "Later, Darcy."

With that, Matilda was gone. Darcy sighed and stared at her desktop background, which was a picture of her and her parents at the beach. White sand, pale purple water, and a blue and white swirl umbrella behind them.

Her watch screen flashed white and a new video chat box appeared. It was Lead Agent Evelyn.

"Hello, Agent Darcy," she said.

"Hello."

"By now, you've had a chance to get to know Ninjastoria?" she asked, although Darcy knew it was not meant as a question.

"Affirmative."

"Your real mission officially starts tonight. Your first task is to take a photograph of one of the thirteen Ghost Vases and then bring it back to us. Your rival team of ninjas will be receiving their mission as we speak."

"Yes, ma'am."

"You have your mission, Agent. Complete it."

With that, Agent Evelyn was gone. Darcy wondered if Serena had been contacted, too, or if she was meant to share the message. She hadn't seen Serena all afternoon.

Darcy sighed. It was time for the real work to begin. She had no clue what the Ghost Vases were or where to find them.

She opened up a web browser on her watch and went to Worldopedia. Nothing. There was very little information on anything related to Ninjastoria. She found an entry on the basic history of the village. There was nothing to be found about any of the wars she had heard about: the Pluton People, the dinosaur assassins, the pixie rebellion. It was as if the ninjas had their own private history that existed apart from the rest of the world.

The only information she could turn up was on Sensei Raheem and his legendary battle with the Mole Emperor. But that had nothing to do with the Ghost Vases, so she didn't even bother to read the article.

She fixed her hair, unplugged her watch from the charger, and went out into the village. She had a feeling that Ninja Steve would know something about the Ghost Vases.

STEVE

Steve was looking at Ninja Kelly's number. Steve was thinking about texting Ninja Kelly. Steve had been doing this for the past thirty minutes.

Since the day she canceled on him, Steve hadn't heard a word from her. She hadn't said a word to him at school, either.

He would type in a message, let his finger hover over the send button, then erase the whole thing. No matter what he typed, it sounded stupid when he read back over it. He needed something cool, something funny. He was getting nowhere.

"Steve!" he heard Nora call. "Steve, your girlfriend is here!"

Steve leaped to his feet and his phone slipped from his fingers. His reflexes were quick, though, and his hand shot out and caught it before it could hit the ground. Steve ran from his room to the front door, where Nora was.

"She's cute," Nora whispered in his ear. "Why's she interested in you?"

Steve ignored his sister and walked past her. Who knew what Nora had already said to her? He'd apologize to Kelly immediately. His sister was a real--

It was Marcy who was standing at the door.

"Hi," she said, with a little wave.

"Hi," he said.

"I wanted to make sure you were all right after Katana Class the other day."

"Oh, yeah, I'm doing fine. I managed to use the right landing maneuver," he said.

"That's something you can learn?" she asked.

"One of the basics. No one's gone over that with you?"

She shook her head. "Could you teach me?"

"I'll teach you!" Nora shouted from the other room and then ran in.

"That's kind of you and I don't mean to sound ungrateful," Marcy said, "but I'd like to work with your brother."

Steve smiled. He remembered when people would knock on the door all the time, asking for Nora to train them. No one had ever come to him. Well, not until now. Steve puffed up, he stood taller, and when he took a step forward he felt like he was lighter than before.

"We need a good place to fall from," Steve said.

"I don't think that sentence gets said all too often," Marcy said.

"It does here," Steve said. "Falling is one of the first things we learn."

In his mind, Steve was going through a series of places. The Raven Tower was a good one for intermediate practice. Chuck's Folly was another, and it had an amazing waterfall, too. Neither of those would do, however, for a beginner.

"Where did you learn?" Marcy asked him, and she tucked a strand of her hair back behind her ear.

"The treehouse in the backyard," Steve said, with a big smile. "Let's start there."

DARCY

Darcy wasn't sure if it would work on Steve.

Serena had mentioned the technique to her, off-hand, after a training session a few months back. It was an ultra-rare moment of semi-bonding between them.

"All I ever have to do, Darcy, is look a boy in the eyes, tuck a strand of hair behind my ear, and smile at him," Serena had said. "If he smiles back, I know he'll tell me pretty much anything."

"That's it?"

"It's so easy, it's ridiculous."

So she had tried it on Steve. He had smiled back. Now he was answering questions that he shouldn't have been answering. Secret stuff. He had told her where the swords of the elders were kept. Had told her that his sister had been a bed-wetter when she was younger.

And now that she had done it, she felt slimy inside. She told herself it was part of being an agent. That, sometimes, you needed to give people a false impression of yourself. It was part of your cover. It was necessary for success and — in many cases —

survival.

She told herself that she was on a mission in Ninjastoria. She reminded herself that rule number three was "Never make friends with an outsider." In the end, she would complete her mission, she would return to the bureau, and she would disappear. She would never see Ninja Steve again. In a way, he would cease to exist.

Still, none of that was helping.

She was up in the treehouse, standing at the edge, and he was standing down on the grass, looking up at her, waiting to watch her fall. He had insisted that she start barefoot, so her shoes were down there next to him.

"Okay, do it like we practiced," he said.

She nodded, flipped into the air, and twisted. She fell and she imagined herself as a set of four arrows branching out from a central point. She rearranged the arrows so they were in a balanced formation and…THUMP. She stuck an ugly landing, hard on her heels. It was too rough to be correct, but it was the first time she hadn't stumbled.

"Nice, Marcy!" Steve shouted, and he pumped his fist in the air. Steve had demonstrated it ten times and it was like he was using multi-boots…only without the boots.

The cheer temporarily made her forget about feeling bad about deceiving him. Until she realized she still hadn't gotten to the real matter at all.

"You know, with my shoes on the ground next to you, it looks like a ghost is standing there," she said.

Steve's eyes went wide and he jumped back. "A ghost? Where?"

Darcy laughed. Steve scowled.

"That's not funny. Ghosts are serious business."

"Oh, come on. It's not like they wander around during the day."

Darcy wasn't really sure about that. The bureau had never provided them with information on ghosts.

"The weak ones don't," Steve said, with a shiver. "The strong ones, though…they're awful."

"So where are they now?"

"The strong ones, the Thirteen, are sealed up."

"The Thirteen?"

"We shouldn't say their names. It feeds them strength, if only a little. Actually, I'd rather not talk about them anymore."

"But now I'm curious about—"

Steve shook his head. "It's not worth it. Ask me about anything else."

Darcy sighed. She felt she had failed again.

STEVE

Later that night, Steve was consumed with the overpowering urge to throw something at Nora. Maybe his dinner plate, maybe the entire table. All he knew was that *something* was going to get thrown.

"Seriously, Steve, you kissed her, right?" Nora said and stuck her tongue out.

"Nora, shut up."

Their parents were out on a mission for the next week. That meant Nora was in charge of the house.

In a way, it was good because Nora was an excellent chef. She had graduated from ninja cooking school in six months, having prepared a grilled octopus dish that made Sensei Chow burst into tears.

Unfortunately, their parents being gone also meant that she'd be around all the time to keep an eye on Steve.

"Come on, little brother, it's okay. You can tell me," Nora said, heaping a scoop of spicy soba noodle salad onto her plate.

Steve used his chopsticks to pick up a square of pan-fried five spice tofu and onions. He did not look across the table. He started to hum. Nora rolled her eyes and continued eating.

Their meal ended in silence. Nora flung the plates, Frisbee-style, into the kitchen, where they landed in a perfect stack next to the sink. Steve threw the utensils so they hit the padded backboard on the wall and plunked into the basin.

Since Nora cooked, the agreement was that Steve would wash everything. He pulled the sponge-sword from its scabbard next to the sink and went to work. While scrubbing the skillet, he thought about Marcy. Did he like her? She was really kind. And there had been that moment when she'd done that thing with her hair that was pretty hot.

Of course, he was starting to wonder if she had also been digging for information. He hadn't noticed right away. The more time he spent trying to teach her how to fall, though, the more she kept asking about other things. Secret things.

"Whatcha thinking about, little bro?" Nora asked. She was standing on the ceiling in her red ninja robes.

"Whether or not I should do my homework," Steve lied.

"I have a suggestion. You should do it," she said.

"Thank you," Steve said.

When he looked back, she was gone. He knew he wasn't

going to do any of his homework. She probably knew it, too. His parents had been called into the school for meetings by every sensei except for Sensei Raheem. Even though he did poorly in Sensei Raheem's History of the Ninja Wars class, he did well in Katana Class, so Sensei left him alone.

Steve was washing the chopsticks when there was a knock at the front door. Then, five more knocks. It was Samurai Sam's "secret" knock to Steve. He dropped the chopsticks, turned off the sink, and rushed to the door. When he opened it, Samurai Sam was grinning from ear to ear.

"Steve, buddy, I have a story to tell you," he said.

"Um…Sam, are you okay? Did you accidentally drink sake instead of water?"

"No, Steve," Sam said. "I'm not drunk."

Steve motioned for Sam to come in. He strolled in, his samurai armor clinking and clanking and making all kinds of terrible noise. Was Sam on drugs? Was he going to have to stage an intervention?

They went to Steve's room and sat down. Samurai Sam's big, dumb smile had only grown bigger and dumber.

"What's going on, Sam?"

"Steve, I think I'm in love," he said.

"Oh no," Steve said. "That's not good. One hundred percent of people who fall in love wind up dead one day."

"Guess who I was hanging out with this afternoon."

"Who?"

"Ashlyn. She came over to the embassy and asked me if I could help her study for the Ninja Geometry test."

Steve lowered his eyebrows. Now, *this* was suspicious. "Oh yeah? How'd it go?"

Sam sighed. "It went so well. We studied, sure, but we talked about everything. Steve, she laughed at all of my jokes!"

Okay, now it was really suspicious. Samurai Sam—best friend or not—told jokes that even Sensei Raheem would have said were corny.

"What did you talk about, Sam? Aside from geometry?"

"She really wanted to know about the history of Ninjastoria. The elders, the sacred katanas, even the ghosts."

The alarm bell blared in Steve's mind. Something was seriously wrong. "Sam, I don't think she's actually interested."

Sam looked at Steve and shook his head. "Don't be

jealous, Steve. Can't you be happy for me?"

"No, Sam, I'm trying to tell you something important. If she was asking you about the ghosts—"

Sam stood up. His face had turned bright red. "You know what, Steve? Never mind. I came over here with good news and you were the first person I wanted to tell. If you're going to be all bitter, I'm leaving."

"Sam, wait, you have to hear me out—"

"No. Forget it. I'm meeting her for dessert tonight and then she wants to go to the Museum of Sharp Objects. It's going to be amazing and I won't let you ruin this."

Sam got up and stormed out of Steve's room. Steve didn't bother to go after him. There was no point, and he'd apologize later, after he'd gotten a chance to explain himself.

He did have an idea, though. Both of the exchange students had come to them, asking about the ghosts. And if Ashlyn had insisted on the Museum of Sharp Objects, there was a good chance that if he followed them on their "date," he'd be sure to find something interesting.

Steve got out his super-stealth uniform—dark as a moonless night, blacker than the blackest ink—and laid it on his bed. When the time was right, he'd go investigate.

DARCY

"I tried the hair thing today when I was talking to Steve. It worked," Darcy said.

"See? Didn't I tell you it was a great one?"

"I can't believe it."

"Boys can be simple. I used it today on that Samurai Sam kid and he told me that the Ghost Vases are stored beneath the Museum of Sharp Objects. Once I found out his dad is an ambassador *and* one of the sponsors of the Museum of Sharp Objects, I asked him on a date tonight. I think he might have fallen in love with me. Isn't that awful?"

"The lying part or the love part?"

Serena rolled her eyes and went back to brushing her hair. Darcy had gone back to hating her. There had been a few moments when she thought it might have been possible for the two of them to be real friends. Now there was this.

Or was Serena the better agent? Was she going to get them farther ahead in the competition? Was it possible that being the best spy meant being the coldest person?

"Anyway, it's time for me to get us on the scoreboard for

this competition. I'm sure I'll have that photo of the Ghost Vase in no time." Serena walked to the door. "It wouldn't kill you to say 'thank you,' you know."

Darcy waved and let Serena go on her way. It gave her time to type some short notes in her diary. Plus, she needed to give Serena a good head start.

Ten minutes later, Darcy headed out the door. If Serena was going to be arrogant about it, Darcy was going to beat her to it. She'd trail them and get the photograph herself.

STEVE

"Hey, Nora?" Steve asked, knocking on the door of her room.

"What, Steve?" she asked as she poked her head out of the door. The latest hit single from Shinobi-Onsay was blaring through.

"I..." he said, and thought he was going to throw up. "I could use your advice on something."

The music stopped immediately. "Well, this is new. Come on in, little brother."

Nora's room was spotless. Her katana stand didn't have a single speck of dust on it, nor did any of her swords. Her shuriken pouches hung from the wall, all of them at the same angle. He knew that if he opened one of them, he'd find exactly thirteen throwing stars in each. Nora claimed it was her lucky number. There was a poster of Shinobi-Onsay singing into a microphone on one wall and her stack of Ninja Seventeen magazines was perfectly organized next to her reading chair.

"What's up, Steve?" she asked, as she sat on the floor and he sat opposite her.

Steve sighed. He told her everything about Marcy and

Ashlyn.

"I might be wrong, Nora, but what if Ashlyn's using Sam to steal something out of the museum?"

Nora bit her lower lip as she thought. "Well, I think you've got a pretty strong case there, little bro. It seems strange to me, too."

"What should I—"

"You know the answer, Steve."

"Right. He's my best friend, I can't let him get embarrassed. I'm going."

Steve stood up and left Nora's room. He went into his own and stepped over the pile of uniforms that needed to be washed. After he changed into his super-stealth uniform, he looked in the mirror and couldn't see himself. If he did everything right, Sam would never even know he was being followed. After all, a key to stealth is having the other person distracted, and something told Steve that Sam would be plenty distracted.

Steve left the house and took Roundhouse Road until it led him into downtown Ninjastoria. Even though tomorrow was going to be a school day, the streets were packed. There were crowds of his classmates outside the movie theatre. The bowling alley had a line going out the door.

Samurai Sam had mentioned getting dessert with Ashlyn. Steve knew that there was only one place Samurai Sam went for dessert. The best place in town. Kickin' Cake.

He looked in the window and saw the display case was full of triple-decker vanilla bean cakes, dragon-shaped choco-strawberry cakes, and an arsenal of cupcakes ranging from their signature Tangy Brightberry to Bitter Moon Chocolate.

The timing was perfect. Samurai Sam and Ashlyn were sitting in a booth, just about done with their dessert.

Then, someone bumped into Steve.

"Excuse me," she said.

It was Ninja Kelly. She was in a new red and white ninja uniform. Very untraditional. Steve liked it a lot.

"It's okay, Kelly," Steve said.

"Steve!" she said, and his heart jumped. "Sorry about not showing up the other day."

"No worries," he told her.

"I wasn't sure how to tell you. My mom has been really

sick. Dad needed me to stay home and take care of my baby brother while he took her to the doctor's office. I'm so sorry."

"You don't have to apologize," Steve said. "You did the right thing."

"I still feel bad, though," she said, "and every time I went to tell you, I thought that you must be mad at me, so…"

"No way. That's not it at all," he said. "I'm not mad."

"Good!" she said, and she smiled brightly. "Anyway, I have to go home now. See you in class tomorrow, okay?"

Like that, she was gone. Steve leaned his back against the window and sighed. He had spent all that time feeling humiliated that she had canceled and that wasn't the case at all. Maybe he still had a chance to hang out with her.

Then Steve remembered why he was out. He glanced back in and saw that Samurai Sam and Ashlyn were no longer at their booth. They were headed for the door and he was right there. He had to make sure they didn't see him.

The shadows weren't particularly thick on the ground, so Steve quickly leaped into the air, flipped, and stood upside down on the awning that ran all around the storefront.

"So, Sammy, is this museum scary at night?"

Sammy? He *hated* being called that. He always said that Sammy was a girl's name.

"Well, not—" Sam started to say.

"I hope so. I love scary stuff," Ashlyn said. "Demons, ghosts. They're so cool."

They wandered away and Steve couldn't hear the rest of the conversation. That was okay, though, he needed some distance. Once they were far enough ahead, he dropped down onto the sidewalk and began to trail them as they made their way to the Museum of Sharp Objects.

As Steve waded through the crowds of his fellow ninjas, he kept noticing a ninja whose hood was on inside out. That was embarrassing. He wanted to say something, but knew that he needed to keep near Sam.

If you could stand in the sky and look down, you would see that the Museum of Sharp Objects was shaped like a crescent moon. The designer, Ninja Vincent, had a thing for the night sky. Looking straight at it, you would see gray, white, and black bricks that made an amazing cloud-like camouflage pattern.

Steve got in line ten people behind Sam and Ashlyn. He could see now that they were holding hands. Steve wanted to be wrong about his hunch. He wanted this to be something good for Sam.

Once he got his ticket, he trailed them as best he could. The first thing visitors saw was a rushing waterfall that fell from the third floor down into the lobby. Etched into the blue marble basin was a relief carving of a katana that, when the water hit, gave the illusion of spinning.

Samurai Sam and Ashlyn had gone to the left, passing under the sign that read "Hall of Really, Really Old Stuff." They used to go there on field trips when they were younger. The hall was filled with tacks that were mostly rust, primitive wooden swords, and a bunch of other displays that never really interested Steve.

The lights were dim and the hallway was winding, so Steve could only see the shadows of Sam and Ashlyn ahead. He stepped very softly, using the Full-Foot Tip-Toe tactic to keep his weight evenly spread with every step.

"…and that's the double-sided sword of Sensei Three-Fingers," he heard Sam say.

"You really know your stuff, Sammy," she said.

"That's what happens when your dad takes you to every museum he sponsors," Sam said.

Steve stayed around the corner.

"I bet you've seen all kinds of cool behind-the-scenes stuff," she said.

"Well, yeah. He gets to see all of the storage facilities in the basement and the exhibit plans before they get finalized."

"I'd love to see something like that," she said. "I love history."

"It's—"

"How about right now? You know how to get down there, don't you?"

"Ashlyn, I don't think that's a good idea."

"Sammy, you're not scared, are you?"

"Well, of course not. It's just that—"

"Please?" she asked. "For me?"

Steve was about to jump around the corner and yell at Sam. The only thing that stopped him was a noise from behind. He turned and didn't see anyone. He could have sworn, though, that he had heard a single footstep. He shook his head and then went around the corner to stop Samurai Sam.

They were gone.

Steve looked all around, trying to find where they had gone. The room was a dead-end. He inspected each display and saw no hint of a door anywhere. Then he noticed a sliver of light that was at the very base of a display case up against the wall. The display contained the earliest known shuriken. It was a brown rock.

Steve felt around for a hidden button. No, that wouldn't be it. That would be too easy for others to accidentally trigger. So where would there be a hidden switch?

The display tag! A small rectangle of dark brass that read, "Belonged to Ninja Chad." Steve found that the nametag could be lifted up. Sure enough, the space beneath it was hollow and there was a single white button.

Steve pressed it and the display case swung to the side, revealing a narrow, dimly lit corridor that spiraled down below. He stepped inside and began to descend as the display case shifted back into place.

After a minute, he stopped, leaped up against the wall, and clung to it. Sure enough, he heard footsteps coming down. He saw that it was the ninja with the inside-out hood. And he was rushing ahead.

Steve dropped down right behind him and put a hand on

his shoulder. "Hey man, what are you doing here?"

The other ninja, to his credit, didn't shout or flinch. He threw a punch and Steve slipped to the side. He dodged a wicked hook and barely had enough time to block the cross that followed.

"Oh. Hi, Steve."

The other ninja, it turned out, wasn't a "he" at all.

"Marcy?"

DARCY

Darcy's training had taught her how to hit fast and hard. Ninja Steve, however, proved to be faster. In this case, it was a good thing. Steve was a friend and if she had knocked him out, she would have felt awful about it.

"What are you doing?" Steve asked.

"I was trying to keep Ashlyn out of trouble," she said, and it was only a half-lie.

"You're not supposed to be here," Steve said.

"And *you* are?" she shot back.

Darcy didn't break eye contact. Looking away first was a sign of weakness. Yes, she was trespassing. Of the two of them, she was far more in the wrong than Steve. Still, she had a mission to complete. And the handbook said that it was okay to break a rule or two if it meant you could complete a mission.

Steve smiled. "You have a point. I'm trying to keep Sam out of trouble. Looks like we're both on the same kind of mission."

She smiled back. He wasn't going to sound the alarm or argue with her. She wasn't going to have to use the stun feature on her watch. He might get in the way of photographing the vase, but at least Steve wasn't going to turn into an enemy.

"We're wasting time," Darcy said, putting on her business face. "Let's get moving."

"I feel like I should tell you that you put your hood on inside-out," Steve said.

She blushed and pulled the hood off. There was no need for it now, anyway. Then, she followed Steve down the steps. When they stopped, they were in a winding hallway filled with steel doors. The place smelled like earth and metal.

The clang of a closing door came from up ahead. Darcy took the lead, passing by doors labeled "Mystic Clothing," "Dragon Pieces," and "Cereal Boxes." The hallway took a sharp turn every few feet. She wasn't sure what kind of crazy person would carve out a jagged hallway, but that was another mystery for another time.

"Marcy, I have to ask you something," Steve said suddenly. "Why were you and Ashlyn asking about the Ghost Vases?"

"It's part of a project we were assigned," she said.

"That's a lie. Tell me the truth."

She couldn't. She couldn't reveal anything. Not even if her life was about to end. That was protocol, plain and simple.

So all she said was, "I wish I could, Steve. No one's going to steal anything, though. I promise."

Steve pressed forward and led them to an open door. It was labeled "Definitely Not Ghost Vases." The one across from it read, "Definitely Ghost Vases" and the one beyond was, "Possibly Ghost Vases."

Darcy went in after Steve and she gasped. Frost glittered on the floor. Icicles hung from the ceiling, some of them bigger than a person. She felt her nose already starting to go numb.

Samurai Sam and Serena were only a few feet away. There was an open crate at Sam's feet and he was reaching in for something.

"Sam, what are you doing?" Steve asked, breaking the silence.

Sam leaped up into the air and whirled around. "What?!"

Serena turned just as quickly.

"You followed me?!" Sam shouted. "What is *wrong* with you?!"

"Wrong with *me*? Sam, you broke into a museum because

a girl asked you to do it," Steve said, his voice thick with anger.

Darcy knew that arguments between close friends were always the worst. She had gotten into one with Matilda once and it had resulted in both of them crying. She wasn't sure if ninjas cried. Maybe they punched trees or wrote haiku instead.

"Sammy, where's the vase?" Serena asked, shivering.

"This crate is empty," he said, turning his attention away from Steve.

"We need to leave," Ninja Steve said.

Darcy knew that what Steve was saying was right. However, winning the contest would be huge. They were so close.

Sam puffed out his chest. "Whatever, Steve." He went over to another crate and pried the lid off. "Aha!"

Samurai Sam lifted up a blue crystal vase. It was the color of the sky in summer. The vase had a million little facets that all began frosting over upon touching the air.

Serena snapped a picture with her watch. So did Darcy. Neither of the boys noticed.

"Now, what were you saying, Steve?" Sam said.

"I said that we need to—"

There was a tremor from above and some of the icicles fell. They sounded like shattering glass. And then Darcy looked up and saw one of the giant icicles break loose. She took three steps and leaped into Steve, knocking him down as the icicle crashed down and smashed into the floor.

"Sorry," she said, rolling off of him.

She looked over at Sam and Serena, who hadn't moved. There was another quake that rattled the room and then the ceiling split open. A flood of weird-looking green creatures came spilling through.

"Mecha-moles!" Steve shouted.

Samurai Sam looked up just in time to have one collide with him. He fell back and the vase popped out of his hands. He fumbled for the vase as he fell, his fingers brushing against it, but not grasping it.

The vase hit the ground and cracked in half. A strange, sparkling mist began pouring out of it, making a sharp hiss. The mecha-moles backed away from the mist and began to cluster together. They dug into the ground and were gone.

Samurai Sam had rolled away. Serena had retreated to

Darcy's side. Darcy looked to Steve, whose mouth was wide open.

"This isn't good," he said. "It scared away the mecha-moles."

Darcy saw what had formed in the mist.

Steve was right.

STEVE

When Steve was five years old, Nora did what all older sisters do at some point. She purposely told him a story that scared him so bad that he cried for ten minutes and then couldn't sleep for ten days. It was, at the time, full of the most terrifying ideas. There was a vampire that looked like a mummy. It could also turn into a ghost. Its favorite food was boys named "Steve." In fact, that was all it ever ate. It drifted from town to town, seeking out Steves, drinking their blood, and wrapping their corpses in mummy rags.

Months later, when Steve was no longer quite as scared of the vampire-mummy-ghost, his parents revealed an even more terrifying truth about the world. Ghosts were real. They weren't bits of mist that came floating through the walls and made funny noises. They were the remnants of angry, vengeful creatures. They were made of white fire and black smoke.

After that, Steve couldn't sleep well for weeks. He would wake in the middle of the night, needing to go to the bathroom, and agonize over whether it was worth it to risk his life by walking down the hall to the bathroom or whether it was better to humiliate himself. Every time, he made it down the hall and somehow avoided death by the supernatural.

These memories came rushing back to Steve as he stood in the basement of the Museum of Sharp Objects. Samurai Sam was still getting up. The vase was still broken.

The ghost sprang out of the broken vase.

Thick mist billowed around the body of the largest tiger Steve had ever seen. It was outlined in sharp white lines, rippling with little white and gray flames that licked the air. Inside, however, it was mostly black, with small slashes of orange. The ghost tiger arched its back and then reached out an enormous paw, examined it.

Then, slowly realizing it wasn't alone, it turned and faced Steve, its large, glassy eyes flickering red.

"Thank you," a slick, hissing voice said, though its mouth never moved.

Steve couldn't have spoken even if he wanted to. Neither, it seemed, could anyone else. The tiger took long strides as it approached them. It leaned forward into Steve's face and Steve could feel the insane heat radiating from the ghost.

"The smell of fear," the tiger mused, pulling back.

Steve licked his lips. His mouth felt like it was filled with sand.

"Well, isn't this strange?" the tiger said, sitting back on its hind legs. "You look just like *them.*"

"Not all ninjas look alike," Steve said, his voice shaking. "That's kind of racist to say."

The tiger laughed, although it almost sounded like wheezing. "I don't think you understand what 'racist' means. Ninjas aren't a race."

"That's exactly what racists say," Steve said, drawing his sword.

"This is stupid," the tiger said. "I'll just curse you and be on my way."

The tiger leaped forward and with one swipe of its paw, knocked the sword out of Steve's hand. The moment the blade hit the ground, it melted into a puddle. A beam of red light shot out from the tiger's red eye and struck Steve in his right arm.

Steve screamed. He screamed because he thought it would hurt. It didn't hurt at all.

The beam faded and then the tiger turned toward Marcy. Steve looked up and saw her frantically pressing buttons on her watch. The tiger did its eye beam thing and it pierced right through it and hit her left wrist.

"Before I leave, I want you to know," the tiger said, looking at Steve, then at Marcy, "that you both look just like your parents."

No one said a word. The tiger turned around, swished its ghostly tail, and walked through the wall, burning a hole into the earth as it went forward. No one was willing to chase after.

"Are you two okay?" Samurai Sam asked, rushing over to Steve and Marcy.

"I…I don't know," Steve said. "I have no idea."

"He blasted your arm!" Samurai Sam said.

"It didn't hurt at all," Marcy said, moving her arm around to demonstrate.

"Then why did Steve scream so loud?" Sam asked.

That was the one question Steve had hoped that Sam wouldn't ask. Now he had asked it.

"It was an over-reaction," he said.

"Oh. Whatever, we should look at your arm," Sam said.

Steve began to roll up his sleeve. He wasn't sure he wanted to. What if he had broken out in a weird rash? What if it was worse than that?

Etched onto his forearm was a single, curving black stripe. A tiger stripe. It looked like a tattoo. He kept rolling up his sleeve until he reached his shoulder, but there was only that one stripe.

Steve glanced at Marcy, who was looking a little pale. Around her wrist was a tiger stripe, too.

"What is this?" Marcy asked.

As she asked it, the museum alarm sounded.

"I think we're going to be in a lot of trouble," Steve said.

DARCY

"You all are in a lot of trouble!" Sensei Raheem barked, standing in the doorway of the museum storage room. The light from the hallway was behind him and it made him look more intimidating than ever.

Darcy looked down at her feet. She had never really been in trouble. Sure, some of her classmates at the Bureau had cheated on tests or sneaked out of the dorms during lockdown. Not her, though. That wasn't her thing. Besides, many of those cheaters and sneaks had been caught and kicked out. That was considered sloppy work.

Except now she was in over her head. She had broken into a museum's storage space. They would force her to go back to the Bureau. Lead Agent Evelyn would be shamed by all of the other agents. Darcy would never be let out on another mission again.

"Of all of the Ghost Vases, Sam, you had to pick *that one* to drop?" Sensei Raheem asked, pushing a finger against Sam's sweaty forehead.

Darcy couldn't help feeling bad for Sam. He had been duped by Serena and now he was taking the blame for a break-in and the release of a ghost. His father, Ambassador Samurai Juan, was standing next to Sensei Raheem, looking down at his son the way you look at a dog after it eats your favorite shoe.

The rest of the museum security squad was running about, although Darcy had no idea what good that could do. The ghost was long gone.

"We're going to take a walk now," Sensei Raheem said. "We have to go to the Security Tower immediately. President Ninja needs to speak to all four of you."

Darcy looked at Samurai Sam as he gave a little yelp and then fainted. He flopped down on the floor and Steve was the first to scoop him up.

"What a terrible dishonor," Samurai Juan muttered as he watched Steve slap Sam back to consciousness.

Darcy glared at Serena, hoping her thought of, "*Look what you got us into!*" would somehow travel, through sheer anger, directly into her brain.

It didn't.

Twenty minutes later, they arrived at the Security Tower. It was not what she expected.

"This isn't a tower," Darcy said.

It was a cottage. A squat, round cottage with stone walls and…a thatched roof. It was more like something you'd find in Knightenberg.

They walked right through the front door. There were no guards.

There was a lone ninja standing there. He wore an olive green uniform and had a full hood covering his face except for a two-inch strip that revealed his piercing eyes. His eyes weren't what caught Darcy's attention, though.

It was the gigantic handlebar moustache…that was somehow on the *outside* of the hood.

"Steve," she whispered. "What's up with that?"

"That's the presidential moustache. It's like a badge," he replied.

"Shut up," President Ninja said. His voice boomed like a cannon.

They shut up.

"Now start talking about the important stuff," he said, twirling the moustache around his finger.

"We messed up," Darcy said, speaking before anyone else could. "We thought we would —"

"Wasting time," President Ninja said, now twirling his moustache with both hands.

Darcy knew she had to create a cover story. And from looking at Serena, she knew that only one of them would be able to do a convincing job of it at the moment.

She balled her fingers into fists. "Fine. I bet Ashlyn that she couldn't get Sam to sneak into the museum. So she got him to think it was a date and then it went from there."

"It was fake?" Samurai Sam asked, looking even more miserable than before.

President Ninja glared at Ashlyn. "Shame on you."

"Thank you, sir," Samurai Sam whimpered.

"Shut up," President Ninja told him, crossing his arms. "Sensei Raheem, tell them about Toran."

Darcy had forgotten about Sensei Raheem. She was still trying to figure out how this was called the Security Tower and how to react to President Ninja.

"Alright, listen up," he said. "Toran the Tiger is the king of the thirteen ghosts. For a while it was Hermes the Clown until Toran defeated him in battle. After that, he kept to himself in the Inside-Out Mountains and the other ghosts left him alone.

"Then, about thirty years ago, Cedric the Rhino and the Haunted Sword of Timothy III challenged Toran. From what we could learn, the battle lasted for twenty years before it spilled over into Ninjastoria. At that point, we had to act. We formed an alliance with our neighbors and went into battle. We thought that by assisting Toran, we could restore order to the ghost world. Instead, he formed a truce with his fellow ghosts and they attacked us. We had squads specifically trained to capture each of the three ghosts. They all succeeded, though not without losses."

President Ninja cleared his throat. "We have to recapture Toran before his full strength returns. We have maybe two or three days before he's recovered from the long term effects of the vase. What more can you tell us?"

Darcy found her voice again. "He recognized me, he said I resembled my parents. Steve, too. Is that an effect of the vase? A foggy memory?"

President Ninja rubbed his chin. "No."

He went to the lone file cabinet in the corner. He rifled through it and pulled out a black manila folder.

"This," he said, handing a photo over to Darcy, "is a photograph of the special team that captured Toran the Tiger."

Darcy could have sworn that her heart stopped. In the picture, standing next to a pair of ninjas she didn't recognize, were her parents.

STEVE

Steve leaned over to see what had rattled Marcy. In the picture, standing next to a pair of non-ninjas he didn't recognize, were his parents.

"Your parents were a team," President Ninja said.

"You know who I am?" Marcy asked him.

"Yes, Marcy, I am fully aware," President Ninja said. "And, apparently, so is Toran."

Steve looked at Marcy. Her parents had teamed up with his? Where could they have been from? As far as Steve knew, The Valley of Fallen Stars didn't train warriors. No one wanted to invade a land that was constantly being bombarded by giant chunks of metal that fell from the skies, so they never needed to defend themselves. No, there was something she wasn't tell him.

"My parents vanished ten years ago," Marcy said. "Did they…was it…?"

Steve could see she was trembling. He put a hand on her shoulder.

"That mission was the last we heard from them," President Ninja said. "I wish I had more to tell you."

Marcy didn't speak. She only stared at the picture.

"So now Toran's loose," Steve said. "He cast a spell on the two of us."

Sensei Raheem's eyebrows went up. "What?! Why didn't you say so earlier?"

"You were too busy lecturing us," Steve said.

Steve rolled up his sleeve and showed his forearm to the others. The tiger stripe had grown thicker. Steve knew he was supposed to be concerned. Except...well, it looked really cool.

"He got Marcy, too. What does it mean?"

Sensei Raheem and President Ninja exchanged glances. The look on Sensei Raheem's face was not a good one. It was the same look Steve's dad would give when Steve told him he had failed a class.

President Ninja broke the news. "It's a life draining curse. Toran is turning both of you into minor ghosts. It takes about two days, although it varies from person to person. Once those stripes reach your neck, you'll become his ghost minions."

Steve felt like he had swallowed fire. A life draining curse was something from stories, not from real life. "You...you mean we're going to die?"

"Sort of," President Ninja said. "There has been scientific debate about it for a few hundred years. I mean, your flesh will slowly burn away in a sea of white fire and then you'll be reborn from your own ashes. You tell me if that counts as —"

"Anyway," Sensei Raheem cut in, "we can stop the curse if we can recapture Toran."

"That's right!" Steve said. "You said in class that you can reverse a ghost or demon curse if the caster is resealed!"

Sensei Raheem smiled. "Not bad, Steve."

There was hope. All they had to do was capture Toran the Tiger. The king of the ghosts. The creature who had fought a battle that lasted for two decades. The more Steve thought about it, the less appealing it sounded.

"I'll get my team together," Sensei Raheem said. "You all need to go home and sleep."

President Ninja cleared his throat. "I'm afraid your usual group is scattered, Raheem. There was an incident in The Mole Republic and we had to dispatch a team a few hours ago."

"Steve's parents? Ninja Darshan? Ninja Georgia?"

President Ninja nodded. "All gone. You're going, too, as soon as this meeting is over."

"You can't send these kids out alone," Sensei Raheem protested. "The Mole Republic can wait until —"

President Ninja held out a hand and Sensei Raheem suddenly sounded as if he had taken a big gulp of helium. Steve recognized it as a level two spell: the spell of balloon breath.

"Raheem, you have your orders. I've sent a message to Ninja Nora. She's our next best ghost expert and she will be here soon. Now, I have other business to attend to. While I'm gone, everyone should shut up."

President Ninja disappeared in a puff of black smoke. Steve breathed a sigh of relief. President Ninja was a terrifying man.

"Why does he say 'shut up' so much?" Marcy asked.

Steve and Sam laughed.

Sensei Raheem crossed his arms over his chest. "President Ninja was a debate champion in college. His patented 'shut up' technique revolutionized the debate circuit here. That's not what we need to talk about, though."

"Yeah, we need to talk about this mission," said Samurai Sam. "Steve's my best friend and this is my fault, so I'm going with him."

"Sam, you have to return home immediately. You must stand trial before the samurai senators and the ninja court. Until then, you are under temporary house arrest," Sam's father said.

"Ouch." Samurai Sam walked over to Steve. "Kick that ghost right in his ghosty face for me, okay? And, Steve, even if you do turn into a ghost, you'll still be my best friend."

"You're the man, Sam," Steve said, and gave him a fist bump.

That left Marcy and Ashlyn. Clearly, Marcy would be coming along. But Ashlyn? What about her?

"This is my fault," Ashlyn said to Marcy. "Let me come along. I'm not going to let you turn into a ghost."

"Are you sure?" Marcy asked.

"Yes. It would kill my record if my partner got ghostified," Ashlyn said.

"Fine," Sensei Raheem said. "You two have some explaining to do, though. Tell Steve a little bit about what's going on."

Steve frowned. Whatever it was, it wouldn't be good.

"Steve, we're not from the Valley of Fallen Stars," Marcy said, wringing her hands. "My name isn't Marcy."

"Oh," he said, not quite sure how to react. "Does it rhyme with 'Marcy?'"

"No! No, it doesn't!" she said quickly.

"Good, that would be too obvious. What's your real name, then?"

Marcy shook her head. "I can't tell you. The rule book says that it's among the worst things we can ever do."

"I've never liked books that much," Steve said.

That got her to laugh.

There was a ninja rulebook. They got it every summer. It was full of "don't" and "no" and "never." Steve didn't understand why it had to be so negative. Or so strict. Most of it was common sense, anyway. He figured her rulebook was probably the same.

There was a knock at the door. Sensei Raheem opened it and Steve saw his sister with an armful of swords, plus some pouches with throwing knives and shuriken. She stepped inside, dropped the weapons at her feet, and got right in Marcy's face.

"Are you the one who got my brother cursed?" she asked, pointing her finger at Marcy's nose.

"No, she didn't. That was me," Ashlyn said.

"When I'm done with you," Nora said, now standing face to face with Ashlyn, "you're going to wish you had been cursed instead."

Steve sighed. His sister could be so dramatic sometimes. "Nora, please don't threaten her."

Nora said, "When someone messes with my family, Steve, I'm going to tear out their —"

There was a blast of black smoke. President Ninja had returned.

"Everyone, shut up."

DARCY

Darcy was pretty sure, by now, that President Ninja was actually a big joke. There was no way anyone would ever put him in charge of anything. Who would ever select such a clown?

"You need this before you go," he said, and held up a blowdart gun and a case that held five thin darts. "If you hit Toran the Tiger with it—"

"It will nullify his ghost fire and make him solid," Nora said, snatching it out of his hands. "Yeah, I know."

"You don't have manners, do you?" President Ninja said. "Fine, steal my thunder. Get going. I have a mecha-mole crisis to deal with, anyway."

Sensei Raheem and Nora led the way out of the cottage. Darcy took a deep breath of fresh air. Then, she felt a tug on her wrist. A slight one.

"Now, we need to know where to go," Nora said. "Since you're both cursed, you're tied to Toran. You should be able to sense where he is."

Darcy and Steve shared a glance.

"He's headed north," Darcy said. "I can feel it."

Steve nodded in agreement. "It's weird, like someone is constantly trying to pull my arm to get me to go that way."

The five of them stood in a circle. Steve, Sensei Raheem, Nora, Ashlyn, and Sam.

"I wish I could come along," Sam said to Steve. "I'm in a lot of trouble, though."

Steve shook his head and gave Sam a hug. "You do what you need to do, buddy. I know you'll be all right."

Darcy couldn't help but smile. Their friendship was something warm, something that you could feel. It reminded her of the friendship she had with Matilda.

"Okay," Nora said. "Sam, you take care of yourself. The rest of you, let's get going."

"I'll come along as soon as I've dealt with the mecha-moles," Sensei Raheem said, and he dashed off into the night.

Nora tossed something to Darcy. She caught it and saw a coin-sized piece of white metal. Was it actually...?

"You have hoverboards?" Darcy asked, as she gave the coin a squeeze.

A sleek black board came soaring over the hill. It was as thin as a sheet of paper, maybe three feet long. Just like the ones

Darcy and Ashlyn had used in training, only black.

"Of course we have them," Nora said. "How else would we get around?"

"I've never seen anyone on one in Ninjastoria," Serena said.

"They're for serious missions, only. Otherwise, everyone would get lazy," Nora said.

Nora handed out more of the control coins. They all got onto their boards and faced north. Darcy wasn't exactly sure how to fight a ghost tiger. But one important fact was clear to her: this tiger had possibly been the last creature to see her parents. Cursed or not, she was going to face him.

"Let's go!" Nora said.

The board responded to Darcy's thoughts and raised up off the ground. The surface of the board turned to gel and her boots sunk in. If she needed to bail, the gel would loosen and she'd be able to jump free.

They took off. The wind kicked up, cool and blustery. Darcy felt the small tug on her wrist. Toran was moving away from them quickly and she wondered if they'd be able to catch him tonight. Did ghosts need sleep? Did they need food?

Serena pulled her hoverboard up beside Darcy's. For a few minutes, they said nothing. Darcy, however, knew that Serena wouldn't have done it unless she had something to say. She was clearly waiting for Darcy to say something first. Darcy had the words in her mouth, could feel the shape of them. But she couldn't bring herself to say anything. She was still angry.

Serena gave up and pulled ahead. Darcy didn't mind being left alone. There was so much to think about, anyway. This was a mess and she needed to sort things out for herself. If only she could have made a list and written out what she needed to deal with. A mental list would have to do. She'd start with--

Ninja Steve had slowed down a little. His ninja hood was up and though his voice was muffled, he was close enough to speak quietly.

"Hey, Marcy?"

"Yes?" she asked.

"I wanted to say that I think it's cool that our parents were a team."

Darcy nodded once. "Now it's our turn, isn't it?"

"Yeah," he said. "Well, that's good because I think you're—"

"Steve! Get back up here!" Nora called.

He shrugged and sped up. Darcy watched him go, wondering what it was he had been about to say.

The landscape changed as they reached the outer border of Ninjastoria. The ground became rocky and rough hills began to pop up. The trees gave way to prickly shrubs whose thorns glowed a pale yellow in the dark. Up above, the moon was a swirl of white and orange.

Nora and Steve began to slow down. Up ahead, beyond the hills, there was a faint light.

After cresting the next jagged hill, Darcy looked down to find that the ground was gone.

Below her were dark clouds, lightning dancing between them, and in the brief bursts of light, all she saw were more clouds, going down and down and down and down.

STEVE

Steve was glad Nora had interrupted him. He had been about to say something extremely stupid to Marcy and Nora had unwittingly saved him. He wouldn't ever tell her, though.

They crossed the border from Ninjastoria and entered Stormistan. It was impossible to miss the transition. You reached a certain point and then — bam! — the ground was gone. Stormistan was all clouds and sky, straight down until you hit the center of the planet. Or…that was the current thought. Those who went deepest never came back. It was assumed that if you tried to descend through a million layers of storm clouds, you were bound to get struck by lightning at some point.

Steve looked down and saw the clouds doing their thing. There were forks of golden lightning, spears of purple lightning, and even swirly green lightning. He thought that it would actually make for a cool date, to come and watch the colors for a while.

They would simply skim over Stormistan as quick as they could to catch up with Toran. It was the fastest way to reach him.

"Nora," Steve asked, "what happens if we do turn into

ghosts? Aside from the dying and being reborn part?"

Nora took a deep breath. "Are you sure you want to talk about this, Steve? Maybe it's better if we don't. You know, we should focus on thinking positive."

"I want to know. Not that I can prepare. I…I'd feel better if I knew. Please," he said.

"I agree," Marcy said. "I'd rather know."

Nora hesitated. When she finally started speaking, her words came out slowly. "Well, you won't ever need to sleep again. You'll be able to fly short distances. You'll burn through pretty much any non-living object with your ghost fire. We have weapons that can hurt you because they're full of magic, but they can't kill you. The only thing that can kill you is another ghost. Otherwise, you'd have to be captured."

"I hate to say it…that doesn't sound too terrible. What are the downsides?"

"On the night of a full moon, you'll be filled with the urge to drink the blood of the innocent."

"Oh," Steve said. "Not cool."

"Okay, we need to get out of here," Nora said. "Full speed ahead, no slowing down until we're out of Stormistan."

They pressed forward, the wind whipping against their faces, and twenty minutes later they were back over solid ground.

Nora called the company to a halt.

"Marcy, Steve, are we headed in the right direction?" Nora asked.

"Yes, we're catching up," Marcy said. "He's somewhere northwest of here."

Steve felt it, too. He looked at his tiger marks and saw that a new one had popped up. At this rate, he was going to be a ghost sooner than they had estimated. He could feel Toran's presence in the distance. The tiger had come to a stop.

"Before we move on, I should probably give you your weapons," Nora said, giving them each two shuriken and two throwing knives. "These are from the special weapons lockers. They've all been made with level three spells. You can't truly hurt or kill a ghost unless you are a ghost, so these will just be for annoying Toran, to distract him."

"No special katanas?" Steve asked.

"The only ones we had were destroyed by Toran the last time he was on the loose," Nora said. "The spell casters who made these died a thousand years ago and no one else has been able to figure out what they did. I've been working on it for a year now without any luck."

"Wow," Steve said. "I had no idea."

"No worries, little brother, I'll figure it out one of these days," Nora said. "Now let's get moving again."

They resumed their hoverboarding and found a narrow dirt path, lined on either side by gnarled, wicked-looking trees.

"Ashlyn, I was told you're an excellent scout. Take the lead," Nora said.

Ashlyn took off. A minute later she came zooming back. "There's a set of tripwires up ahead. Follow me."

Sure enough, stretched between the trees at various heights and angles were razor-thin strands of steeltanium. Even up close, Steve had trouble seeing them. If they had kept up their pace, they all would have ended up with broken bones and busted hoverboards.

After slowly making their way above, below, and around the wires, they made the group decision to travel on foot for a little while. Nora was the first to deactivate her hoverboard.

"This seems to be the safest way," she said.

"No!" said Ashlyn, but she was too late.

When Nora touched her foot to the ground, a giant coiled spring shot up and launched her into the air. Nora went flying one way, her board went another, and the blowdart gun for fighting Toran went straight ahead.

Nora twisted in midair and landed on her feet. The hoverboard hit the ground with a thump. And the blowdart gun landed in the outstretched claw of a camouflage-colored robot.

It was a small robot, maybe three feet tall. Its head was a triangular flatscreen monitor, its body was shaped like a bowling pin. There were three arms, one on each side and one in the center. At the very base of its body was a single sphere that it rolled around on.

"Thanks, chumps!" he said and sped off.

Ashlyn was the first to run after it. "Follow me!"

Steve and the others deactivated their hoverboards and ran after her. She hopped over more tripwires, ducked under another. It was then that Steve realized how keen her vision was, and *that* was what made her an excellent scout. Steve couldn't move as fast, but he could pick out where she had jumped and where she had ducked.

The robot knew where every trap was, too, and it zoomed along, occasionally popping up into the air or collapsing down into a smaller shape.

They followed in pursuit until they came to a clearing. There was a small village of cottages and they seemed to be having some kind of festival. A drum was beating. There were bright lights and there were people out and moving. There was even a big bonfire.

The robot disappeared among the celebrating people.

As Steve drew closer, he realized that it wasn't a celebration at all.

The village was on fire.

DARCY

White flames.

Right away, she knew it was ghost fire that was consuming the village.

Darcy tried to keep her eyes on the robot, who was wheeling away with their only chance at capturing Toran the tiger. There was too much commotion, though, to keep track of him. The village was burning, people were panicking.

The roof of a nearby hut burst into flames. A man leaped out of the doorway and landed on his stomach. He rolled in the grass and started screaming.

"Hey! It's okay!" Darcy told him.

The man, who was wearing plaid pajamas, yelled, "Tell my kids I love them! Tell my wife I hate her!"

"You aren't dying," Serena said. "You aren't even burned."

The man's eyes went wide. "What? I could have sworn the ghost was on me."

Darcy and Serena shared a look. The man began to cry.

Darcy patted him on the back and told him to find a way out of the village. Then, the girls resumed looking for their target.

"Hey!" Nora shouted. "We found the ghost!"

They followed the sound of her voice. Several people were running in the opposite direction, bumping into them and nearly knocking Darcy over. When they found her, she and Steve were busy trying to draw the ghost's attention. It was a gorilla.

She watched as Steve threw a shuriken at it, but it wasn't one of Nora's special weapons. It sailed harmlessly through the gorilla's silver and purple body. White flames danced along its giant forearms and in the middle of its chest was the letter "G."

It didn't look good: the gorilla had cornered the robot against a barn wall and the robot was clutching the dart gun.

"Robot, you have listen to me!" Darcy called.

The small robot chirped out something nonsensical. Then, its monitor flashed with the word, "HELP" in bright red letters. The gorilla began to hover in the air. The robot shrunk its leg-stalk down and began rolling from left to right.

"Here, robot, robot, robot," the gorilla taunted, in a voice that sounded like a beating drum.

"Throw us the blowdart gun!" Serena yelled. "You can't even use it! You don't breathe!"

The robot shook its head. It said, "Can't afford to lose it."

"Can you afford to die?" Darcy said.

The robot considered. Then, it used one of its three arms to catapult the blowdart gun over the gorilla's head. The gorilla watched it sail through the air and it landed in Darcy's hands. She quickly pitched it to Nora, who was already pulling out one of the darts.

"What is that for?" the ghost gorilla asked. "Weapons won't hurt me."

Nora puffed out her cheeks and shot the dart. It hit the gorilla with a *thwack* and stuck right in its chest. The gorilla looked at its chest in shock. It howled and tried to rip the dart free.

The ghost fire on its forearms began to sputter. The gorilla floated ten feet off the ground and then came crashing down.

"So...heavy," it said, trying to get up. "What...is this?"

"It's called gravity," Steve said. "It's a law that most of us have to obey."

All around them, the ghost fires died, then went out.

Puffs of purple smoke drifted away. The village quieted down. People began returning. Soon, they surrounded the gorilla.

"How did you wake up?" one of the villagers asked. "We sealed you away, Grummo."

The gorilla still couldn't get up. "Toran did it."

A murmur spread through the crowd.

While Grummo was talking, Darcy noticed the robot was beginning to inch away. She tapped Steve on the shoulder and pointed. The two of them made their move and caught the robot between them.

"Where are you going, robot?" Darcy asked.

"Running away after we saved you?" Steve said. "That's bad manners."

The robot lowered its monitor head. It flashed on both sides, so both Darcy and Steve could read it.

"Sorry" it read, in purple, curly letters. Then, in green, "Thank you."

"Why did you steal from us?" Darcy asked.

The robot beeped sadly and said, "I need to trade to get batteries for mom."

Darcy felt her heart sink. Even though she wasn't entirely sure if robots had mothers, the tone of the robot's words had struck her.

"What kind of batteries?" Darcy asked.

"XS-57," the robot screen read. "2 of them. She's running very low."

Darcy popped open the back of her watch. The watch had a compartment for extras. She took both of her spares and slowly approached the robot.

"Darcy, those are super expensive," Serena said.

"If it can help someone's mom, I don't care," Darcy said.

The robot's monitor flashed pink. "Thank you. My name is Augustus Septimus Droidon."

"My name is Marcy. Good luck to you, Augustus," she said. "And please stop setting traps for travelers. It's rude."

With that, she placed the diamond-shaped batteries into one of Augustus' hands. He lifted the batteries close to a camera in his chest and then he spun around once. A tiny side compartment popped open from his leg stalk and he deposited the batteries in there. He sped off into the night.

Darcy turned back to the center of the village, where Nora

had taken charge.

STEVE

"Steve, go help them pick up the coffin!" Nora commanded.

Steve rolled his eyes and joined close to twenty men and women of the village. They moved in a single-file line over a hill to pick up the magic device that had kept their ghost sealed for all those years.

Grummo was still losing his fight to gravity. Steve couldn't wait until the same thing happened to Toran.

The coffin was smaller than Steve expected. Four feet long, two feet deep. It was solid black, except for a thin, golden line that went in a wave from the very top to the very bottom.

"Why do they need twenty of us to carry it?" Steve asked.

No one answered him. They each grabbed hold of a metal handle on either side. Steve found a spot toward the end.

A woman counted off, "One, two, three."

They lifted. Steve grunted. The coffin must have weighed several hundred pounds.

"What is this thing made of?" Steve asked.

"Steel, titanium, and steeltainium," one of the men said.

"To keep anyone from running away with it."

It took ten minutes to carry it back to where Nora was. Steve was left feeling worn out, as if he had finished up one of Sensei Raheem's legendary workout sessions.

The gorilla had struggled to his knees and was beginning to crawl. "This is humiliating. What a terrible poison."

"Yeah, well at least nobody set your house on fire," Nora said. "We're going to put you right back in it."

"Wait, don't," the gorilla begged.

They put the coffin down next to Nora. She sat on top of it, cross-legged. Steve had heard that Nora's true gift was in dealing with ghosts. This was hard to prove, though, as most of the ghosts had been subdued long before she was born.

She touched a finger to the wavy gold line on top and it began to pulse with light. She kept one finger on the line and touched another to her heart. Her chest filled with a golden glow. Then, she pointed her hand away from her heart and a beam of light shot out. It spiraled around Grummo. The gorilla shimmered, then shot straight through the side of the coffin and disappeared with a *pop*.

Nora hopped off of the coffin. The villagers cheered. Steve

clapped.

His sister came back over to where he was. She brushed her hand across her forehead. "I'm glad that actually worked."

"What?"

"We could only practice on minor ghosts in class," she said. "I wasn't sure if I'd have the strength to bind a middle ghost."

"Well, you looked calm out there," he said.

Marcy and Ashlyn came closer and congratulated Nora. The villagers offered them all a feast if they stayed. Steve's stomach growled. A feast sounded perfect.

"I know this is bad manners," Nora said, "but we happen to be on a quest right now and time is very important to us."

One of the villagers, a tiny old woman, stepped forward with a basket in her hand. "Please, take these fruit buns."

Nora accepted the gift. "Thank you so much. We wish we could stay and help."

There were cheers as they left the village. Even though their houses had caught fire, they still had something to cele-brate. They had triumphed over a ghost.

"What happened to the robot?" Steve asked. He was hoping to find it, chop it up, and turn it into a television.

"We helped him out and he left," Marcy said.

"*You* helped him out," Ashlyn said. "Maybe."

"No need to be sour," Steve said. "If she helped, she helped. That's good enough for me."

Nora nodded. "Now, let's get going."

Steve pulled out his hoverboard coin and pressed. Theirs all arrived in seconds, except for Nora's, which had a little catching up to do.

"Let's go get that tiger!" Steve said.

He rolled up his sleeve and gulped when he saw half of another tiger stripe had already formed. He looked over at Marcy and showed her.

"We have plenty of time," she said.

And even though he knew it wasn't true, hearing her say that made him feel better.

DARCY

"I only have one and a half stripes, too," she said quietly to Steve, and it was a lie.

She didn't like lying. As a child, she had sworn that she wouldn't tell lies like the adults did. They said things like "This won't hurt" or "It'll only be another minute" and it was always a lie. Lying to give hope, though, was what she had done. Steve was looking worried and Darcy tried to make it better.

They didn't have a lot of time, though.

When no one was looking, she had checked.

Her stripes were already halfway up her arm.

She tried to ignore the thought as they skimmed through the outer edges of Knightenberg and saw, in the distance, the castles with their drawbridges up. Humongous gray and red stone castles, bristling with flags and alight with fires in the watch towers. She had read about Knightenberg and its fiefdoms. Some of the other agents were interested in the warrior knights with their mecha-horses and rocket-lances. She was more interested in the fact that some of the people lived in castles while the rest were left to live in huts.

Luckily, the people had brokered a truce with the Glass Dragons and it had held for nearly a decade, so at least they no longer had to worry about them.

Serena edged closer to Darcy, while Steve was up ahead with his sister. "So, Darcy, how are your stripes?"

"I'm not looking," she said.

"Maybe you'll have a stripe or two left over when this is all done," Serena said. "That'd be pretty rad."

Darcy laughed. "Maybe."

"Are we close?"

"Yeah. Toran has been in one place for a while now. I wonder why he stopped."

"We'll find out soon," Serena said. "And when we get that tiger with the dart gun, I'm going to give him a good kick in the ribs for what he did to you."

Darcy was shocked by the sincerity of it. "Thank you," she managed.

A bright, full moon crept out from behind a tuft of clouds. Nora cursed.

"Ghosts are stronger under a full moon," Nora warned

them. "This is not good."

Darcy suddenly felt very hungry. When Nora tossed the basket of fruit buns to her, she and Serena each took two of them. The golden brown dough was light and squishy. Inside was a rainbow-colored jam that was sweet and tangy. Darcy wasn't full, though. And she didn't particularly like how sugary the jam was. She wanted something more, something with a darker, deeper flavor. But that would have to wait.

Darcy and Steve took the lead. They closed in on Toran's location. Nora announced that they were reaching the edge of Knightenberg, where the Glass Dragons' land began.

"He's waiting in there," Steve said.

They approached from high ground, looking down over a wide field of white grass and stubby black flowers. Up ahead was an oval-shaped arena made from marble. The gates were square and the one closest to them was wide open. Darcy saw enough seating to hold several thousand people and, for some reason, a light-up scoreboard. A giant torch basin sat at either end of the arena, both of which were lit with white ghost fire.

Darcy clenched her hands into fists. She gritted her teeth together. The tiger curse was growing stronger, she could feel it. Steve was brave enough to look directly at his stripes. She told herself that she was going to be brave enough to ignore her own.

"Everyone, get up here," Nora commanded.

They gathered close. Nora stood up extra straight and pointed at the arena. "That is where knights have their seasonal tournaments. The best of the best fight there."

Steve cleared his throat. "Why are you telling us that?"

His sister smiled. "Because tonight, we're going to be the best of the best. We have to be."

Nora brandished the dart gun. "There are four shots left. All it takes is one hit."

"How about Steve and I go in through the gate, while you and Ashlyn find another way in?" Darcy said. "Maybe you can get a shot off before he even realizes you're there."

Nora nodded.

"I'll use my multi-boots to climb up and over one of the walls," Serena said. "But what can I actually do to help?"

Nora said, "Stay back and watch and hold onto this Ghost Vase. If everything goes right, you'll be able to hand me the vase at the right time. If everything goes wrong, we'll need someone to report what happened."

"But—"

"That sucks, I know. You have to do it, though," Nora said.

Nora and Serena took off in different directions, leaving Steve and Darcy on a path to the main gate. They were silent for a few seconds as they stared ahead at the gate. Darcy knew that the next ten minutes would determine the rest of her life. She didn't want to become a ghost. Not yet. She had just found out that her parents had worked with the ninjas of Ninjastoria. There was so much more she needed to know.

"We're going to be fine," she said, though she wasn't sure she believed it.

"My sister is the best shot in the entire village," Steve said. "Everyone knows that."

"Right," Darcy said.

Steve edged his hoverboard closer and took her hand in his. Their eyes met for a moment and Darcy blushed. Steve did, too.

They entered the arena.

STEVE

The hallway they traveled down was chilly and dark. The white glow from their hoverboards splashed their shadows across the walls like charcoal-colored paint. Steve held onto Marcy's hand, trying not to squeeze too tightly. For all he knew, this was going to be the last time he held anyone's hand. He didn't want to let go.

The reality was that he had to. As they reached the tunnel's end, they stopped their boards and left them propped against a wall.

"We have to go out there," Steve said.

"But you don't want to," she said.

"Not really."

"I don't, either," Marcy said, and she looked down at their hands. She finally said, "Let go on three?"

"On three," Steve agreed.

The numbers echoed in his head as she spoke them. "One, two, three."

And like that, they let go.

As he walked out onto the field, he saw the tiger, burning bright, like a white sun. Steve tried to clear his head, to focus on the ghost tiger that he would probably be fighting in a minute, but all he could think about was the fading warmth from where she had been holding his hand.

Then he noticed there was someone else with Toran. Someone wearing a long, dark coat and a gray mask with three red slashes on the left cheek. Someone who was definitely not a ghost.

The man looked at Steve and Marcy. "Hello again. Good to see you're still alive."

Steve had no idea what to say. Marcy did. "What are you doing here?"

The masked man said, "I had to make a deal."

"Who are you?" Marcy asked. "What do you want?"

"I wish I could tell you more," he said, then looked at his watch. "I'm just about out of time, though."

He touched his watch and neon blue ones and zeroes started spilling out of it like a fountain. They puddled at his feet and he slid straight down into the ground.

What had just happened? Was that some wizard magic of

Knightenberg? And how did Marcy know him? Steve opened his mouth to ask her.

Then Toran growled.

The ghost smirked. His fire danced in coils along his tail and his ears. He sat back on his haunches and began to let his tail drift back and forth.

"Look at you," he mused. "Bravely chasing—"

Toran turned, mid-sentence, and with a swipe of his tail fire, obliterated the dart that would have stuck in his flank. He roared and the stadium walls shook. Then he leaped into the stands.

Instinctively, Steve drew his sword, then remembered that it would melt the moment it touched Toran.

He saw the ghost pounce and then a black-clad figure rolled out of the way, smooth as could be. The tiger swiped a massive paw at Nora, who used the lightning step technique and disappeared in a flash.

"What do we do now?" Darcy asked. "We're useless."

They watched as Toran chased after Nora, his claws coming dangerously close to turning her into ribbons. She weaved through the stands, slipped out of his range, or side-stepped at the very last moment.

Steve held one of the magic throwing daggers in his hand and took aim. He didn't know any advanced techniques. All he could do was throw a dagger or a shuriken and hope that it didn't miss.

Steve waited until Toran was circling Nora. Steve threw.

Steve missed. The dagger clattered against a seat in the stands.

Toran rolled into a ball and then sprung at Nora. She clapped her hands together, touched her fingers to her cheeks, and breathed out a cloud of red and yellow flames. The spell of dragon breath. It was strong enough to catch Toran in mid-air and knock him back.

"Quite the spell," Toran said, impressed. "That must have taken a lot out of you."

Nora was tiring. Steve could see it, plain as could be. The ghost would never run out of energy, especially under a full moon so bright. He stood there, helpless, and he watched Toran drive Nora toward the center of the arena, never giving her a moment to catch her breath or use a technique, let alone aim the dart gun.

"I'm bored now," Toran said, his tail twitching.

"Nora, get out of there!" Steve shouted.

He took two strides and leaped. Nora rolled to the right and Toran, without landing, changed his direction.

Of course, Steve realized. He's a ghost. He isn't bound by gravity. He's been tricking her.

Nora let out a horrified shout as she must have realized the exact same thing.

Steve yelled for his sister.

The tiger bared his fangs.

DARCY

There was nothing she could do. Darcy stood, anchored to the ground, as Toran attacked. She realized she was about to watch someone die and her stomach felt like it was tying itself into a knot.

Then there was a flash of metal. A dagger struck Toran's tail. He snarled and turned away from Nora, looking for his attacker. Darcy looked behind her.

"Pull it together, agent," said Lead Agent Evelyn. She was in full combat gear: thin black body armor, titano-silk gloves, and rocket boots.

Toran growled and floated up into the air. "What was that?"

Lead Agent Evelyn let out a single laugh. "Something newly invented. It's a spirit metal designed to hurt ghosts like you. It also absorbs ghost fire."

"How annoying." The tiger craned his neck and pulled the dagger out of his tail. His teeth flashed with orange fire.

His tiger ears twitched and he spun and batted away another dart from Nora. Only two were left now…

The moon slipped behind a bank of clouds. Evelyn put on a silver face mask and ran forward while his head was turned. She tossed a package back behind her that landed at Darcy's feet.

Darcy scooped up the black bag and opened it. Inside were three katanas.

"But there are four of us," Darcy said, and looked just in time to see Evelyn toss a sheathed katana to Nora.

She handed one of the red-handled katanas to Steve and marveled at how light it was. Whatever spirit metal was, it felt like it was barely there.

"Who is that?" asked Steve.

"I can't tell you that. I can only tell you that she's on our side," said Darcy.

"How'd she find us?" Steve asked.

"Probably tracked our watches," Darcy said. "They're embedded with—"

"Hey! Throw me a sword!" said Serena, as she came running toward them.

Darcy tossed a sword to her and watched as Serena ran to join Evelyn and Nora, who were keeping Toran busy with a flurry of attacks.

"Let's go!" Darcy shouted, and she and Steve dashed in, as well.

Toran, who was surrounded, flew straight up into the air and looked down at them all. Evelyn activated her rocket boots and went after him. The tiger dipped below her and the spirit dagger she threw missed the mark.

Evelyn turned as quickly as she could and threw another dagger that sliced against the tiger's side.

Toran howled and crashed down onto the arena floor. Right in front of Nora, who had the dart gun pointed straight at him. She fired and there was no way she could have missed.

The tiger caught the dart between his teeth.

Darcy gasped.

He then spat the dart onto the ground and swiped his paw at Nora. It struck her forearm and she dropped the dart gun. Her sleeve immediately burst into flames. Nora yelled and fell back. With a single movement, she tore off the entire sleeve.

"Well now," Toran said, and picked the dart gun up in his mouth. He crunched it into pieces.

Darcy, Steve, and Serena surrounded Toran and began to attack. Darcy knew she didn't have Evelyn's armor, though, and had to keep her distance. Even so, she sensed that the tiger was only playing with them.

Evelyn flew in and Toran delivered a back kick that shot her straight into the stands, flaming like a comet until her armor kicked in and extinguished it.

"You're almost out of time," Toran said.

Darcy felt her arms burning from swinging the sword. It had felt so light at first, though now it felt like her muscles were on fire every time she swung. And then Darcy had a terrifying realization.

Her arms *were* on fire.

The curse was nearly complete.

She was becoming a ghost.

Which, according to what Nora had told them, meant one very important thing: she was the only one who could truly fight Toran.

STEVE

"Marcy!" Steve yelled. He saw her arms turn transparent, then completely white. He watched the flames begin to ripple along them.

She didn't hear him.

Instead, she tossed her sword aside and walked toward Toran. Steve sent one of the magic shuriken flying in. It nicked Toran's cheek and a bolt of lightning came down and struck him, stunning the ghost.

He needed to drive the tiger back. Marcy had clearly given up, but there was still time to break the curse — she wasn't a full ghost yet. He readied his second magic shuriken and…

Marcy punched Toran square in the face. The ghost leaned back on his hind legs and she threw a right hook that caught him on the side of the neck. Then she leaped up and threw an uppercut that made the tiger fall on his back. Steve was impressed, to say the least.

"Did you kill my parents?" Marcy asked, as Toran got back on his feet.

DARCY

Darcy clenched her fists. "The last time anyone saw them was when they came to confront you! What happened to my parents?"

The tiger stretched. "I didn't kill them. Now I wish I had."

The ghost fire that had spread across her body wasn't burning nearly as hot as the fire in her chest. He was supposed to give her answers. He was supposed to tell her something that would put an end to her wondering.

Evelyn swept in and landed next to Toran. He quickly flicked his tail and the impact sent her spinning away. Darcy was on her own again.

Toran smiled a toothy grin. "The last I saw, they were sealing me, alongside the ninja boy's parents. If I had killed them, I never would have wound up in that vase."

Toran snarled and leaped at her. She held up her ghost-fire arms and she caught his forelegs. The force of it caused her to slide backwards even with the enhanced grip of her multi-boots, her heels digging up the ground. Darcy let go and, with a deafening shout, threw a walloping punch that caught Toran on the side of his face.

The clouds drifted and she felt the light of the full moon coursing through her, how it gave her more strength.

She wondered if it would be enough.

STEVE

"Steve, we have to do something big," Ashlyn said, suddenly appearing at his side. "And we have to do it quickly. Think!"

In the corner of his vision, he saw Marcy fighting the tiger, toe-to-toe. She was throwing a flurry of punches and it still wasn't enough to drive Toran back. A new ghost, no matter how much she tried, wouldn't be able to defeat one that was thousands of years old.

Nora had recovered and regrouped with them. "There's still one dart left on the ground. We need a plan to--"

Before Nora could finish, Steve took off, running. Steve wasn't about to let Marcy turn into a ghost. He still had too many things to tell her.

Without losing speed, Steve plucked the fallen dart out of the ground. "Marcy, get out of the way!"

She glanced back. She dropped flat on the ground. Steve leaped over her.

Toran opened his mouth and a blast of fire shot out. Steve swung the spirit metal katana, and cut the ghost fire in half.

Steve yelled at the top of his lungs and threw the dart as

hard as he could. It cut through the air and landed in the top of Toran's head.

The tiger's ghost fire began to sputter. He began to claw at the air. Then he collapsed. At the same time, Steve saw that Marcy's arms began to turn back to normal.

He ran over to her and put his hands on her shoulders. "Are you okay?"

She nodded slowly.

Then, Steve hugged her.

DARCY

She hugged him back.

Her arms were hers again. It was a strange thought to have.

When Steve let go, she rolled up her sleeve and looked at her skin. Her right arm was completely normal again. On her left shoulder, however, two of the tiger stripes remained, inky black. She swallowed, hard.

"Oh no," she said. "What about you, Steve?"

Steve rolled up his sleeves. He still had one stripe on his forearm, though it was much more faded than hers.

"Why do you think there's still one left?" she asked.

Steve shrugged and said. "Probably because the dart made Toran weaker, but it didn't kill him."

Darcy saw Nora walking over to the tiger, who was behind Steve. Ashlyn threw her the Ghost Vase. Nora immediately started the ghost sealing ceremony.

The tiger spoke up. "I made a deal before you got here. I let you seal me away."

Darcy shivered. Steve laughed.

"He's lying," Steve said. "He's messing with us one last time."

And then, before anyone could ask any questions, the ceremony was complete and the tiger was gone, sealed away in a vase, just as he had been before. Nora took a wobbly step, touched her hands to her forehead, and then sat down.

Agent Evelyn was standing beside Serena. She waved Darcy over.

"I'll be right back, Steve," she said.

Evelyn gave a rare smile. "Good work, agent."

Serena said, "You were amazing."

The comments made Darcy feel warm, though not at all like being covered in ghost fire. It was a good warmth, a gentle warmth.

"Who was the tiger talking about making a deal with?" Evelyn asked.

"Do you remember the masked man?" Serena said.

"The man who showed up the night we got our mission assignment," Darcy added. "He was here."

Agent Evelyn's smile vanished. She punched a quick message into her watch. "We need to go now."

"But we need to go back to Ninjastoria—" Darcy started.

"Your mission is done. Someone will retrieve your belongings. We're going back immediately," Evelyn said. "That's an order."

Darcy looked over at Steve. She ran to him and flung her arms around him.

"I have to leave now, Steve."

"But can't you—"

"My real name," she whispered. "It's Darcy."

"No, wait, I haven't—" he started, but Darcy knew that if she stayed any longer, she'd lose her resolve. Before he could finish, she took off running.

Agent Evelyn hooked an arm around Darcy's waist, the other around Serena's, and her rocket boots fired up and shot them into the night sky. As they flew away, she looked down at the arena and waved goodbye.

She wondered if she'd ever get to see any of them again.

"Well, that was dramatic," Nora said. She was carrying Toran's new vase with one arm, her new katana in another. "They could have at least said a proper goodbye."

Steve nodded. He was looking up at the empty sky where Marcy — no, Darcy — had been. Now she was gone. So was Ashlyn, or whatever her real name was. Steve wondered how Samurai Sam would react when he told him they took off into the night and vanished.

"Steve? You there?" she asked. "I need you to help out with the extra hoverboards. The girls took their coins, so we'll have to carry the boards. I don't want to chance dropping this vase."

"Yeah, sure," he said. "Understood."

He wasn't supposed to feel this way. They had contained the tiger, they had reversed the curse, no one had died. Yet he felt hollow. He felt like he had lost.

He clicked his coin and his hoverboard came speeding back over to him. Steve was about to step onto it when Nora began laughing.

"Oh no," she said. "This is too good. Is my little brother

heartbroken?"

"No," Steve said. "It's not like that. It's like—"

"You don't have to explain," Nora said, and winked. "I get it and I'll let it drop."

He smiled, then set about finding the missing hoverboards. Darcy's was where she had left it when they stepped out into the arena. Nora pointed him in the direction that Ashlyn had gone in and soon enough he found her board, sitting on one of the empty bleachers. Thankfully, the boards were made of a super lightweight material, so carrying both of them was no problem.

"You were tough out there," Nora said, when he got back to where she was. "You've got nothing to feel bad about."

"I—"

"She was from the Bureau of Sneakery, Steve. That's how they operate. They go in for a mission and then they vanish. It isn't personal. And, trust me, after you stabbed a ghost tiger with a magic dart and stopped the curse, I don't think she's going to forget about you. Now, let's get going. We can stop back in that village for a proper meal this time."

"I'd rather go home," Steve said.

So they did. After hoverboarding until sunrise, they made it back to Ninjastoria. They entered at an official checkpoint, a black building with black windows. The ninja guards scanned their shuriken to confirm their identities. When they saw the new swords and tried to scan them, their machines went haywire.

"It's a prototype," Nora said. "I'm sure if you check our records, you'll find that President Ninja himself sent us on this mission. He'd want us bringing our new weapons back."

The guards conferred and agreed to let them in with their possessions.

"Welcome back," one of them said.

Steve breathed a sigh of relief. It was good to be back in familiar territory. It felt right to be back in the land of Tae Kwon Donuts and the mirror maze and the Museum of Sharp Objects. The other places out there were...well, pretty strange.

As they got closer to their house, Steve felt his stomach rumbling. The last thing he had eaten was one of those fruit buns. He thought that a big bowl of spicy ramen would be amazing, or maybe some pan-fried hamburger dumplings with ketchup, or, no, fried chicken fried rice.

Standing outside the front door, Steve caught the smell of

something being fried. That meant that his parents were back, another good thing.

Nora opened the door. "Mom? Dad? We're back."

The ninja in their kitchen, however, was not who they were expecting.

"Come on in and shut up," said President Ninja.

DARCY

One week later, Darcy and Serena sat across from Commander Natalya, who had finally returned from her mission. She was dressed in an olive suit that had her Commander stars pinned on her left sleeve, at the shoulder. Glancing at the stars made Darcy think of the two tiger stripes that were still on her left shoulder. It had been three days and they showed no signs of fading. Not that they hurt. Or burned. Or felt any different from the rest of her skin.

For the past hour, they had given Natalya their side of the story. The recording would be analyzed, compared with Lead Agent Evelyn's, and then encrypted in their secure database.

"Most first missions don't end up like this," Natalya said. "The goal was to give you something just beyond your skill set. Instead, you two wound up going toe-to-toe with an ancient spirit, with your lives on the line. So don't worry about the fact that you lost the competition to the ninja exchange students."

Natalya tapped the top of the table and a smaller screen between Darcy and Serena blinked on. A fuzzy photo of the masked man appeared. It was taken from the time they had encountered him in the lobby.

"Moving on, do either of you know who this man really is?" Natalya asked.

Both girls shook their heads.

She said, "If you catch any trace of him around the bureau or on any of your future missions, your primary objective will change. You will abandon the mission and immediately contact the Bureau."

Darcy studied the picture. There wasn't much to go on. The coat was oversized, the mask completely covered any facial features.

"If he is so dangerous, shouldn't you tell us something about him?" Serena asked. "We're always told that the more information you have, the better."

Natalya tapped the table and the image disappeared. "All I can tell you right now is that his name is 'Three.'"

Darcy spoke up. "Does that mean there's also a One and a Two?"

"Thank you both for your time. You are dismissed."

Darcy bit her tongue. To press any further would be stepping out of line. Actually, what they had done already was way out of line. Darcy knew that her old self never would have tried to get more information out of a Commander. The handbook clearly stated that their word was final. But that was the old Darcy. The new Darcy realized that once you had survived a ghost curse, you were far less afraid of breaking the rules. Once your arms had broken out in ghost fire and once you punched a ghost in the face, your view of the world was going to change.

"You been okay?" Serena asked, when they were on the elevator tile. "I haven't seen you at the mess hall lately."

"I've been feeling exhausted," Darcy said. "I've been sleeping a ton and I keep missing the regular meal times."

It was a half-truth, so she didn't feel awful.

"Okay, well if you're up at a normal hour tomorrow, let me know and we'll get breakfast," Serena said.

"I will," Darcy said. "And thank you for asking. I mean it."

The tile reached the lobby. The old woman who sat behind the stone desk smiled warmly at them and waved. They waved back and left.

"Darcy, if something's bothering you, please don't keep it a secret forever, okay? I know you and I haven't really been the best of friends, but I'm starting to worry about you."

"I can't talk about it right now," Darcy started.

"Is it boy stuff? I promise I won't make fun of you if it is," Serena. "You know, nevermind, I shouldn't pry. Tell me when you're ready, okay?"

"Okay," Darcy said, and the girls parted ways.

The campus was mostly empty at eleven at night. Darcy wandered back toward her dorm. She stopped off at the café to see Matilda. However, the door was locked and a sign was posted that read, "CLOSED."

With nowhere else to go, Darcy went to her room. Her bed was unmade. Her closet was a mess. There was a pile of her dirty clothes in one corner. She took off her watch and put it next to her pillow. She didn't even try to write in her diary. All she wanted to do was lay on the bed.

Serena hadn't guessed right. It wasn't about a boy. Well, she did miss Steve. He had been kind and funny and brave. That kind of thing wouldn't leave her bed-ridden, though. At least, she hoped that it never would.

No, that wasn't it.

Darcy lay on her bed, on her side. The fingers on her right

hand touched her left shoulder, where she knew those hideous tiger stripes were. She hated them. Serena had tried to convince her otherwise. She said that it was so cool that she got to have tattoos when none of the other agents were allowed.

She rolled onto her back and stared at the ceiling. Then, she raised her left hand and examined it. It looked the same as always. It was her hand. And yet…

Darcy raised her left hand. Darcy snapped her fingers.

One by one, all of her fingers were coated in white fire. Then the fire spread to her palm, where it bloomed into a fiery flower.

Darcy snapped again and the fire went out. She shuddered, pulled the blanket over her head, and closed her eyes.

STEVE

President Ninja slammed a platter of shrimp tempura down onto the table and then fiddled with his moustache. "Eat up, kids."

Nora and Steve were still standing by their front door. Steve was trying to figure out why the president was in their house.

"Where are our parents?" Steve asked.

"They're dead!" President Ninja said. He put down some forks and chopsticks. "Not really! They're on a new mission, scheduled to be back tomorrow morning."

Then, he took a few pieces of shrimp for himself and sat down at the head of the table. "Come on, it's my grandmother's recipe."

They left the hoverboards at the door. Nora carried Toran's vase over, put it on the table, and they both sat down. Steve's stomach growled. He piled his plate high with shrimp. Nora did, too.

"Welcome back," President Ninja said. "Thank you for subduing Toran. Also, thank you for not dying. That would have looked bad."

"You're welcome," Steve said, while stuffing his face.

"The Bureau of Sneakery informed me that you came into contact with a masked man. Is that correct?" President Ninja asked.

"Yes," Steve said.

It had been so brief and the fight afterwards had been so fierce that Steve had forgotten about the man.

"Should you ever come into contact with him again, your mission is over and your only priority is to report back to me."

"What? How is that--?" Nora began.

"Shut up," said President Ninja. He straightened out his moustache and stood up. "I'm leaving now."

He marched to the front door, picked up their hoverboards and turned. "I need the coin keys."

They tossed him those and then he disappeared, leaving them with a tray of tempura shrimp and a million questions. Steve looked at Nora. She shrugged and helped herself to more food.

"He's the president we have, Steve. We have to accept that, weird as he is," she said.

They did the dishes together. Then, a heaviness came over Steve. His eyelids felt like they were made of solid steeltanium. Nora looked just as tired.

"In the morning, I'm going to see how Samurai Sam is doing," Steve said.

"That's fine," Nora said. "Something tells me that you won't have to go to classes for a few days. After a big mission, you tend to get a few days off."

Steve went to his bedroom and shut the door. He lay on his back and stared up at the ceiling. He wondered what Darcy was doing. He wondered if he'd ever get to see her again.

Before his thoughts could get too deep, however, he drifted off.

When he woke in the morning, the smell of pancakes was filling the house. He heard bacon sizzling in a pan. Steve went into the hall. Nora came out of her room at the same time.

President Ninja was back in their kitchen. "Good morning and shut up."

They sat down and sighed. Not again.

"Bad news, kids," President Ninja said. "Your parents have been captured. Sensei Raheem, too."

Steve put his head down. Nora gasped.

"You want eggs with your pancakes?" President Ninja asked.

THE END

A NOTE FROM THE AUTHOR:

Hi there! Great to see you here! There are so, so many stories out there that you can choose from and the fact that my book somehow made it to you is amazing to me. Thank you for reading it.

I'm a new author and this is my first novel. I would absolutely love it if you could take a minute or two and post a quick review on Amazon.

Even if it's one or two sentences, every Amazon review that gets posted helps more readers discover Agent Darcy and Ninja Steve.

My fans are my favorite people and I love hearing from them. You can always contact me through my website, and while you're there, you can check out the latest blog posts or sign up for the Ninja Newsletter to get special updates on Agent Darcy and Ninja Steve.

Thank you for being awesome!

-Grant

P.S. Book two, *Robot Rumble*, is out! It picks up right where you just left off.

Acknowledgements

Writing a book is a long, intense process. It takes so, so many people to make a book into something you can actually hold, and they all deserve thanks.

My parents made sure I had a never-ending supply of books when I was growing up. They are the reason why my imagination is as strong as it is. They've read many copies of many manuscripts that have gone nowhere. For some reason, though, they keep asking me to send my latest ones their way. Maybe it's love or something?

I call my brother, Chad, every other day (and, sometimes, every day). He teaches classical trumpet, conducts for several performing groups, and leads an amazing music ensemble in San Francisco called Elevate Ensemble. He constantly reminds me — even if he doesn't always say it — that art and creativity are always worth the struggle.

The cover art was designed by Tristan George. Tristan is one of those guys whose creative talents just blow you away. He was producing a *storm* of sketches and ideas from the moment we started working together. I thought it would be close to impossible to end up with a cover that matched the character images in my head. In a matter of weeks, Tristan managed to prove me utterly, completely wrong.

Jonathan Flores helped me figure out how to publish with Amazon. He was the best mentor I could have hoped for.

Years ago, my friend Jared accepted my challenge to do NaNoWriMo. That was my first time writing 50,000 words, and while that original manuscript may never see the light of day, our weekly editing sessions propelled me to the finish line and showed me that I was capable of writing long works.

Thank you, Jared.

Ryan laughed out loud when he read some of the lines from this story, which gave me hope that not all of my jokes were terrible.

My test readers did a phenomenal job of helping to fine-tune this manuscript.

I also need to thank my students and the members of my creative writing club. Without them, I never would have created these characters and sent them on an adventure.

ABOUT THE AUTHOR

Grant Goodman teaches middle school English
in Montgomery County, Maryland.

He is fueled by Ray Bradbury stories, spicy curry, and 9:30
Club concerts.

Agent Darcy and Ninja Steve in...Tiger Trouble! is his debut
novel.

You can follow him on Instagram: @grantgoodmanauthor

CPSIA information can be obtained
at www.ICGtesting.com
Printed in the USA
BVOW03s2202131117
500348BV00001B/27/P